THE
WORLD
IN
BETWEEN

Maisie Tasset

Amazon Book Publishing Center
420 Terry Ave N, Seattle, Washington, 98109, U.S.A

The opinions expressed by the Author are not necessarily those held by Amazon Book Publishing Center.

Amazon Book Publishing Center works with authors, and aspiring authors, who have a story to tell and a brand to build. Do you have a book idea you would like us to consider publishing?
Please visit amazonbookpublishingcenter. com for more information.

Dedications

The book is dedicated to my family.
Thank you for your support and believing in me.

Acknowledgements

I would like to thank Ms. Debbie Jenkins for her support along this journey
and encouraging me to write and publish an entire book.

To my Mom and Dad, thank you for believing in me and your excitement
along the way as I wrote each chapter. Tehgan...thank you!

— CHAPTER 1 —

I woke up groggy and tired. Gray fog stood in front of my window. Wisps of cold air could be seen swirling outside my window. I poked my head out of my bedroom window and stuck my head into the clouds. I felt like I could fly away. I laid back down on my bed and checked my phone. The clock read 8:00 a.m.

"SHOOT! I'M LATE FOR SCHOOL!" I scrambled out of bed, threw my pajamas off, and struggled to find an outfit. Once I found one suitable for the school's strict dress code, I quickly dashed out of my bedroom into my mom and I's small apartment.

"MOM!!" I yell at her from the small hallway that's not really a hallway. "What is it?!" She jumped and hustled around the stove.

"Why didn't you wake me up!" I panted.

"Well, sorry Sage, I thought you had an alarm."

"By the way, it's Saturday," My mom looked at me with a sly smile. I woke up early for nothing!

"Oh-my-gosh, really mom?" I let out a slight laugh and head back to my room to clean and put on some jewelry and a more casual outfit.

I walked out of my bedroom, seeing that my mom had left for her brunch with her boyfriend Jake, who I really didn't like. I walk to the bathroom to brush my short brown hair and style it. I just had it cut, and I love the way my hair drops onto my shoulders. I headed out of the bathroom and back to my room, eyeing my mom's messy bedroom. I got my phone and walked back over to her room. I started picking up her clothes and making her bed. I was startled when I suddenly saw a small lump moving under her sheets. Our landlord doesn't allow pets in his apartments unless they are emotional support or a guide dog.

I lift the covers and see a small black kitten rolling around under the sheets, playing with a loose thread. The kitten seemed strange in a way. It gave me a feeling of mystery and uncertainty. Its hair was dark black with a few gray hairs. It had human-like eyes that appeared to be a deep blue color.

2

I scurry to the kitchen, leaving the kitten on the bed to try and find milk. I found the cabinet of baby formula my mom always keeps in case she finds a cat on the street. I walked over to the bed, and the kitten was gone. The bed was made almost perfectly, and the window was closed. I checked under mom's bed to find the cat, I looked behind pillows and in the bathroom.

To my surprise, the kitten was gone.

My mom walked back through the door holding Jake's arm. They walk in laughing and head right to the couch.

"Hey, Sagie!" Jake always calls me that and it drives me insane. I try to be as polite as I can,

"Don't call me that," I said that through an awkward smile and gritted teeth.

"Are you oka-" Jake says, getting cut off by my sharp footsteps moving away from him.

"Honey, are you okay?" Mom stood up and headed over to the non-hallway-hallway to talk.

"Mom?"

"Yes, honey, what is it?" She had a concerned look on her face and pushed away a stray hair on my forehead. I looked behind her and saw Jake watching the TV intently. What a surprise, he was watching football and muttering words he probably wouldn't teach me, as per usual.

"So, today, I saw your bedroom all messy, and I picked everything up because I wanted it to be a nice surprise, a-a-and after I made your bed, There was a cat, w-w-well, more l-like a black kitten under your sheets a-a-and I went to get some milk and w-w-when I came back it was gone and the bed was made again I-I-" at this point, I was stuttering and a mixture of scared, and confused.

"Hmm," mom thought hard and long before she talked to me again. "Mom, please, don't tell Jake," I said pleadingly.

─── CHAPTER 2 ───

It became cold and dark outside. My mom went out to dinner with Jake, so it was just me in the apartment. I put some milk out in case the kitten came back. I cooked up some warm soup and brought it over to my bedroom when I saw the small black fluff ball on top of my bed.

"Oh really, how did you get up there!" I picked up the cat and placed it gently on the floor. It still seemed strange, and a soft breeze flew into my bedroom. I walked over to the window to close it when I saw it was already closed. I whirled around to find the cat, but instead, I saw a girl standing in front of my door.

"WHAT THE~!" I let out a bursting scream.

"SHHH!" The girl came running over, clamping her firm hand over my mouth. My eyes were shocked once I got a good look at her. She had short curly hair, fair skin, black ripped jeans and a striped tank top. *Who is this?*

"Who are you!" I tried not to yell, but it slipped out like most of my words.

"I'm Ivy, who are you?" She seemed fascinated by me. She scanned me up and down and started pawing at me as if she was a wild animal.

"I'm Sage, but could you not~" I put my hands up and stepped away from her.

"Oh my gosh, yeah, I am so sorry. Sometimes I am a cat on the inside and a human on the outside, it's annoying."

I let out a small, relieved breath. *"She might actually be kinda cool"*. The front door creaked open, and I heard the footsteps of mom and Jake. Kinda weird they came back at 7:30.

"Who's that ugly, walking brick?" I'm surprised that Ivy thought Jake was ugly, most people say he's a *beaut*. Whatever that means.

"That is Jake and the short woman next to him is my mother," I whispered so my mom couldn't hear. She glanced at me, peeking behind my wall and started walking toward me.

"Shoot! Ivy hide...u-u-under.. I-I-in my closet, NOW!" Ivy scrambled all around my room, trying to find the two sliding doors on the wall.

"Honey, is everything okay here?" My mom walked in with a concerned look on her face.

"Yep, everything's totally fine," I barely managed a straight face.

"Hmm," Mom scanned my room and walked away. The floor creaked behind her.

"That was a close one." I opened the closet door, and Ivy was gone. There was no trace of her. I checked the time, which read 7:35 pm. In a bit of a daze, I walked into my bathroom and saw the kitten sitting on top of my counter. "What are you doing? I thought you left!" I whispered loudly.

Meow. All she did was cock her head to the side and meow at me.

"Well, are you gonna change into a human or-?"

Before I knew what was happening, a thick black swirl of smoke was rapidly spinning where the cat had been sitting just a moment earlier. It looked like a miniature tornado was about to take out my bathroom. Just as quickly as the swirl started it faded, and Ivy was sitting on my counter in human form. She sat there slightly leaning forward with her hands gripping the counter and her legs crossed with a sly smile.

I turned just in time to see my mom standing in the doorway with her mouth hanging open in shock.

"What is going on here?" Mom asked in a shaky voice.

My mom stood there, white as a ghost. "Mom, you don't look so good. Let's take a seat." I shuffled quickly to my room, pushing mom over to my bed so she could sit down.

"Sage! Who's that!" Mom yelled.

"Uh-" I wasn't sure how to answer that question. I told mom what I had seen up until this point. Ivy was now standing near my window, looking out onto the street below, lost deep in thought.

"Can Ivy stay in my room for tonight, remember, I have an extra mattress from the trundle bed that I had," I said as I looked at mom with pleading eyes.

I looked at Ivy, who had a smirk on her round face.

"I know where I can stay."

"Oh! Okay, and where might that be?" Mom asked her.

"Hold onto my hand," She held her hands out to mom and me. I grasped it and it felt like a cloud, soft and a little strong. Wind started blowing around us. I got very dizzy and then everything went black. We woke up in a cold world. I was surrounded by green mountains and... "DRAGON!" I scrambled to my feet and tried to find Ivy and my mom.

"Ivy!" I yell for her.

"Sage!" I heard her call back.

"Where are you~" I whipped around and saw they were right behind me. "What is this place?" I asked as Ivy came in for a hug.

"This is *my* world," she said.

"Excuse me, er, Izzy, right?" Mom looked as if she might throw up.

"Uhm, Ivy, what's up?" She knelt down next to Mom, who was doubled over, holding her stomach.

"Where's the bathroom? Or SOMETHING I CAN SPEW IN!" Mom freaked out and started gagging.

Ivy helped mom up and held onto her until she was steady on her feet. Once mom and I were able to focus on our surroundings, we saw a magical village lush with trees, plants, and flowing rivers like nothing we had ever seen before. The trees were so high they looked as if they could touch the sky. The plants were bright vibrant colors that seemed to have flecks of glitter all over. We had never seen anything so beautiful. In a daze, we started walking down the hill towards the village below.

"TAXI!" Ivy waved her hand dramatically while rubbing moms back.

"Oh, Ivy! Nice to see you here!" A young lady with strange-looking ears waved to Ivy.

"Hi Marly, no time to talk now," Ivy stopped mid-sentence.

"Wait, could I come over because my friends here just came from Earth and feel a little woozy." We started walking over to the woman.

"Oh, of course! How would you like to get there?" Marly set down a basket full of bread and pointed her finger at the road, and many types of vehicles appeared.

"I think carriage- or what would be fastest?"

"Oh, the broom, for sure." Marly walked over to the cluster of vehicles and pulled out a long broom. "I don't think that's safe, given my health right now," Mom said gruffly.

"We'll take the carriage, thanks." We walked over to a white and gold carriage. Ivy and mom got in first. Of course, I was the last one because I was admiring the thing.

"I haven't seen one of these in a while!" Mom looked almost emotional.

"My dad—your grandpa; had a beautiful top-of-the-line carriage, and we would ride everywhere in it." "That's amazing mom! Have you been here before?"

"Yes, but that's...uh...story for another time," Mom smiled.

* * *

"Ahem, we're here." A flat voice said from the front of the carriage.

Marly's house looked like a house you'd see in a fairytale. It was a small blue cottage with white trim along the windows, the door, and outlining the roof. Darker blue shutters complimented the already amusing windows.

"Wow!" I slowly stepped out of the carriage, finding myself on the ground because I missed the steps.

"Oh my gosh! Are you okay!" Ivy came running out of the vehicle and knelt down next to me.

"Yeah, I'm fine," I quickly fixed myself and brushed off some street grime when I realized my shirt ripped.

"Ugh! My clothes are ripped! I looked down at my torn-up clothes.

"Don't worry, I have some extra." Ivy smiled at me and started walking toward the house.

As I walked along the path, beautiful flowers and small ponds filled the yard.

We stepped inside, and we both were taken back by the beautiful twisting stairs leading up to three bedrooms and a lovely indoor balcony.

"Follow me," Ivy waved her hand toward me and mom. She led us into a bathroom, which was for mom, and a bedroom like mine, for me.

"Here are some clothes you pick!" Ivy swung open her doors to her huge closet.

"Woah..." I was speechless. I ran around giggling the whole time, running my hand along all of the amazing clothes Ivy had.

"May I recommend something?" A soft British voice said at the door. The lady looked around my mother's age.

"Oh! Sure!"

"Ivy, Darling!" The aged lady called. "What is it, mother!"

"Is it okay if I recommend an item of clothing to your good friend here?" The woman gave me a soft smile.

"Of course!" Ivy said, walking back into the bedroom.

Ivy's mom walked slowly into the closet and picked up a blue layered dress you'd see maids wear.

"Mother, I don't think Sage wants to wear my old dress," Ivy walked in and put the dress away.

"I will find an outfit for her, thank you, mother," she pulled out a nice pair of fluffy pajama shorts and an oversized t-shirt.

"What time is it, though?" I asked as Ivy handed me the clothes.

"It's around six thirty." She looked out to her bedroom and looked at a wonky clock above her bed.

"That's an odd little clock," I said.

Meow.

"Oh, have you gone back to cat form?"

Meow. Ivy shook her head approvingly.

"Oh," I was kinda disappointed I couldn't spend a night with human Ivy.

"Boy, am I beat!" Mom walked into the living room where I was sitting, looking out the window.

"Hi, mom!" If you want, I can show you the bedroom you'll be staying in.

"Well, shouldn't we be heading back?" Mom came over and sat next to me.

"NO! I wanna stay here! It's amazing! This place is like the amazing small town you'd see in movies and in your dreams! We can't just leave!" I slapped my hand over my mouth.

"The portal closed once you guys got here, it'll open back up when the next visitor comes." Ivy's mother stood at the entryway of the living space.

"And when might that be?" Mom tried to be polite.

"Whenever someone opens the portal again, dear, it's really that simple!" She walked out with her long night dress flowing behind her.

"Dinner at seven!" Marly walked in the door with a sing-songy voice.

MEOOOOW! Ivy's black furry body raced down the stairs, sniffing the bread that was in Marlys's basket.

"Oh! Ivy, why are you a cat at this hour? Don't you want a proper dinner with your friends?" Marly picked up the fluff ball and cuddled her close.

Meow. Ivy ran upstairs on her four legs, soon to be running back down with only two.

"Here, I will show you to the Dining Room," Marly picked up her basket and walked into a beautiful and rustic dining room with food already made.

"Who made the food?" I was very impressed.

"Well then, let's all sit down, and I will give you all of the wonderful details of this new town." Marly ignored me.

"Well, our world is called Drakengard, the most common pet in our world is a newt or a wyvern, only trained! Our common vehicles are the scooters and the carriages. We have some strange people here, like me. I am a fairy," Marly presented her pointy ears.

"Mistress Binna is a shapeshifter along with her daughter, Ivy, and we have werewolves, wizards, and elves. The list goes on!" Marly paused and looked me directly in the eyes.

"It's a beautiful little village, although we do have lots of bad weather and a really great school!"

Marly continued with more information about the land and the people. We all finished our delicious food and got ready for bed.

"We were hoping that if you came with me from New York, you might want to stay and learn more about...yourself," Ivy smiled.

"I don't understand," I replied.

"But you know, if you do decide to stay, you can't go back, at least for a while," Ivy explained.

"What?" I asked.

"There's a process for staying here," Ivy said.

"You have to undergo a trial to become one of us..."

"One of us? One of who?" I asked, still very confused.

"Are you ready to see what the *witch* will give you?" Ivy walked into our room, holding a tub of popcorn.

"I don't know, I don't like the fact that after I do this, I can't go back home." I was sitting on a bean bag reading a book.

"I don't really wanna talk about it right now," I shifted in my seat. "Oh, Well, would a movie help?" Ivy asked sympathetically.

"Uhm, I guess?" I responded. "So, what movie?" I asked.

"I don't know, we can see what's on," I got excited after she said that.

Ivy turned on some LED lights that lined the room as well and set them to purple. "So, what movie?" I asked.

"Uhm, what about *Enola Holmes*?" Ivy sounded excited. However, I've never heard of it before. "Oh, sure!"

Ivy turned on the TV with a regular human remote that connected to a regular human TV.

"Finally, something *normal*," I sighed and leaned back into the bean bag.

"What, do you think that we don't have TV's?" Ivy looked over as she kept clicking on the remote. "Well," We laughed.

We turned on Enola Holmes and laughed and laughed about random things.

* * *

After a few weeks passed, it was around the time when I had to get "creaturefied," as Ivy called it. I had learned more about the people, the land, and all of the *magic* that I can't explain.

After breakfast, we walked over to a surprisingly big building that was very fancy. The whole lot of us, Mom, Ivy, Marly, and Mistress Binna, kept walking down the long stone hallway that led us to a massive room which had a small fogged up window and two rows of wooden benches, and a small bed lay in the front of the room.

"Uhm..." I swallowed hard.

"Don't worry! Everything will be okay," Marly put a warming hand on my shoulder and gave me a soft smile.

A tall, old lady slowly walked out of a door holding a large book in her right hand and a wand in her left hand. A shorter woman stumbled out of the door, holding a minty green gown on a plush pillow. "Well, this'll be fun." Tears started to fill my eyes and Ivy rubbed my shoulders.

"Miss Sage Caitlyn, please step up onto the bed." The small woman yelled. Her words echoed across the big stone building.

"Here is your gown, walk through that door right there to put it on." The small woman added. I looked back at my mom and my friends, and they looked very, very happy. That was a feeling I lost right as we walked through the giant wooden doors.

I walked over to the door and opened it. The room was small and smelt of old wood. A plush stool sat in the corner. A small kerosene lamp sat on top of a wooden table next to the stool. I held the gown in front of me, scanning its mint green fabric.

Hey! *Maybe it's green for me!* I tried to be positive.

I put on the gown, the fabric felt soft against my skin, I started to feel wobbly on my feet. As I stepped out from the dressing room, my vision started to cave in on itself and the corners of my eyes started to lose sight. Two figures stood by the bed, and my friends sat on the wooden benches.

A few candles lit a path to my bed, which looked so cozy and inviting.

"Sage, please lay down."

"Sage, Please close your eyes."

It felt like time had slowed down, life going just a bit slower. "Sage, wake up, please."

I could hear voices speaking to me, but I couldn't make out who was saying what just before I lost consciousness.

CHAPTER 3

"SAGE!" Wavering voices surrounded me. "Sage, please wake up!"

"Please, Sage!" Many, many voices surrounded my bed. People shook me. I woke up with a sudden jolt.

"PLEH!" Someone poured water on my head.

"Who are you guys?" I had also lost my memory. And everything seemed fuzzy.

"Sage!" a girl with curly black hair held my hand. I pulled away from the stranger.

"Sage, do you really not remember us?" A tall, youthful woman walked over to me while a shorter, older-looking woman stood sobbing.

"Don't touch me!" I hopped off of the bed and looked around. "Where am I?" I started to hyperventilate.

"Okay, dear, let's take you to the hospital," A tall older woman took my arm, and the curly-haired one grabbed my other arm, lifting me off the ground.

"NO! LET ME GO!" I squirmed and kicked and yelled to try and get out of these strangers' firm grasp.

We arrived at a small hospital, but when we walked in, It became massive. Almost like magic.

The strangers set me down once we walked in. A Blue lady sat at the front desk typing on a computer.

"Ah, Binna! What brings you in today?" The blue lady said, looking at Binna with her big black bug eyes. I assumed she was an alien.

"Sage Caitlyn here has seemed to have lost her memory while being "*creaturfied*" Binna said, patting my shoulder.

"Well then, I will bring in our finest doctors!"

"There we were in what seemed to be a waiting room. Amongst us were different creatures of all sorts, reading magazines and sitting in the same chairs as us. The scene reminded me

of some fantasy movie that showed a bunch of aliens at a barbershop, minding their own business, waiting for their turn..."

"Sage Caitlyn." A tall woman with white hair, snow-white skin and soft red eyes stood in a tall doorway.

"Right this way, please!" She walked over to my seat and gave me a soft smile. A small gust of wind swirled around me when I stood up. I looked around for the doctor, but instead, saw an arctic fox standing at my feet.

"The doctor is a shapeshifter, don't be alarmed." The front desk lady said. I started following the doctor-fox when a group of people barged through the door, all looking toward me.

"SAGE!" The same group of people in the large building before were now here. "Who is Sage's mother?" The front desk lady said, putting her blue arms up.

"I am." a short woman with dirty blond hair tied in a bun emerged from the crowd, holding up her hand.

"Okay, please follow Doctor Winter," The Blue lady pointed to the Arctic fox standing before me.

"Uhm.. okay," my *mother* started walking toward me.

The other people watched us, their mouths parted.

"Whatcha looking at?" I snarled at them.

I looked over my shoulder and noticed that my mom was also gaping her mouth at me!?

"Darling, I think your body is glowing green!" Mom explained in between stutters, her body shaking from the horror.

"Was I turning green? I don't know. But one thing was for sure and that was that I was feeling embarrassed. It was just too many eyes on me and I totally freaked out".

"Uhm." I manage to squeal a small sound, feeling exceptionally embarrassed at this point.

"So, uhm. Anyone wanna show us the rooms?" I said with traces of humiliation and hope in my voice.

—— CHAPTER 4 ——

When we got to the room, , a hospital gown lay on the bed with a note saying to put it on. Once I put the gown on and settled down, the doctor had a very serious face.

"Sage, your power is something no one has seen for ages."

"No wonder you lost your memory! Your gift is so powerful you're lucky it didn't kill you in the process of getting it!" Doctor Winter huffed and stood up off my hospital bed, rubbing her temples. "What's gonna happen?" I asked.

"We are going to have to send you to an institution."

"It's like a school for girls and boys like you," she said ominously.

"You'll have a wonderful time there." Dr. Winter walked over to me with a sly smile.

"So, what?" The curly-haired girl named Ivy asked me.

"Well, they are going to send me to an institution for kids like me," I rolled my eyes.

"Oh my god," Ivy started to cry.

"I'm shipping off tomorrow, so I better pack," I sighed and walked toward the door. When we returned home, I walked to my bedroom and started packing up.

"Hey, Sage?" Ivy walked into my room. She looked downcast. "Yes," I walked out of my closet, holding an arm full of shirts.

"I hope that your memory comes back, and I hope you have an *okay* time in the nuthouse." she let out a small chuckle-sob.

"Well, thank you," I continued packing.

"Now, could you leave? I need to be alone,"

"You sure? I could help-" Ivy walked over to me.

"I SAID, PLEASE LEAVE!" A sharp ringing hit my ear. "AHH!" I fell to the floor, holding my ears.

"Sage!!" Ivy dropped to the floor and rubbed my shoulder. "Are you okay?" she looked me in the eye.

"I'm fine," I get up instantly and brush myself off. I walked back to my closet to finish packing.

"What do you want for your dinner, Sage?" Binna walked into my room.

"Ivy, let Sage be. She has a lot going on right now," She walked into my room, escorting Ivy out.

"If I have a lot going on, how about you leave as well? I have to pack anyway, right?" I looked up from my suitcase lying on the floor.

"I was just asking what you want for dinner, but," Binna looked offended.

"I'm sorry, it's just, I can't remember anything, and this new power is terrible, and I have to be sent to an institution, and everyone keeps trying to help me when I don't need help and talk to me when I don't want to talk," I choked back tears.

"That is understandable. I would feel the same if I were in your shoes," Binna came and sat next to me.

"Well, do you know anything about the school?" I looked up at her soft, wrinkled face. "Oh! Well, uhm- no, no, I don't," She stood up and grinned at me.

"Dinner is Chinese food. I hope that's okay-" A tall young woman entered my room.

"Oh! Sage! I had not even a second with you! How are you doing? Also, if you forgot who I am, I'm Marly Banks," Marly shook my hand.

"Chinese food! That's my favorite!"

"Oh my gosh! I remembered something," I whispered under my breath. "What's that?" Marly turned her face sideways, cupping her pointy ear. "Oh, nothing," I smiled.

The following day was dull and cloudy. I woke up to the sound of a car horn outside our house.

"SAGE CAITLYN!" Someone was pounding at our house's door, yelling my name. "Coming!" I quickly hopped out of bed and rushed to the door.

"Oh-" It was a worker at the institution.

"What are you wearing?" The worker sneered at my oversized clothes.

21

"I just woke up, sir, what do you expect? A ball gown?" I laughed at myself.

"Put your knickers on at once! And grab your bags! You're already wasting time," He waved his hand behind me and stepped into the house uninvited.

"Could you at least tell me your name?" I asked as I started walking toward the stairs. "Doctor Raylon," He lifted his chin and tugged on his white button-down.

"Now, get your bags! Enough dilly-daddling," His sharp gray eyes followed me up the stairs. "Sage, going so soon?" Everyone walked into my room.

"I have to go, speed hugs!" I gave everyone a quick hug.

"Okay, I have to get ready; otherwise, who knows what will happen." I walked to my closet and put on jeans and an oversized T-shirt.

I got my luggage and hauled it down the stairs while my friends and mom followed behind me.

"Perfect, now, hop in the bus," Doctor Raylan opened the door for me, and I saw a purple school bus that read "Sir Theodore School for the Gifted " on its side. And small windows lined the top of the bus.

I grasped my suitcase handle tightly.

"Goodbye! Bye!" Everyone stood in the doorway waving to me and crying.

"BYE, MOM! BYE IVY! GOODBYE EVERYONE!" I waved to everyone while tears rolled down my face.

Doctor Raylan opened the van door, and I saw many kids in seats as well.

"Geeze, save it for the funeral!" a boy sitting in the middle row in the middle seat said rudely, narrowing his coffee-brown eyes at me.

"Excuse me?" I tried to find a seat.

I walked along the side aisle, trying to find an empty seat.

"Looks like you're stuck with me," A red-haired girl said, patting the seat beside her. I threw myself down onto the gray seat.

"My name's Garcia, what's yours?" She seemed nicer than the boy, so I decided to trust her. "It's Sage," I said quickly.

"Who's the boy?" I asked.

"Oh, him? That's Ezran, the *school's* most popular guy, but he's also the meanest. If you're new, don't expect you guys to become besties."

"And there's like a million girls that like him. According to my research, the chances of him asking you out is"... Garcia pretended to tap into an imaginary calculator... " ah, zero".

"Wait, this is a school?" I asked her.

"Yeah, you didn't know that?" Garcia looked at me like I was crazy. "Is it still an institution?" I asked, confused.

"No."

"The school is called *Sir Theodore: School for the Gifted*."

"They call it gifted, but what they mean is absolutely crazy."

"Are you really gonna go and make friends with this sort?" Ezran shook his head and walked over to Garcias and my seat. His fluffy brown hair draped over his face when he leaned.

I opened my eyes wide and blushed.

"She's a year one! Let her be!" Garcia shooed him away.

"Well then, looks like you'll be alone for the dance," He smirked at me and walked away. He wore a white button-down, red sweater vest, a burgundy blazer, burgundy dress shorts, black socks and black shoes.

"Wow," I watched him return to his seat and pull out a book. I couldn't quite make out the title. "Do you seriously like that guy? He made fun of you the second you got on the bus, girl!" She drew my attention back.

"Oh, me, liking him? I don't think so."

"Also? Are there uniforms?" I looked down the bus aisle and saw everyone wearing dark red clothes.

CHAPTER 5

After we got off the bus and got our luggage, a massive mansion sat upon a grassy hill with a surrounding fence and gate in front of it.

"Welcome, everyone! I am Headmaster Louis," A tall old man stood before the bus crowd.

"And I am Dean Beatrice, head of the girl's wing called Florence, named after the founder of the girl's wing." Dean Beatrice said softly, her friendly gaze washing over the girls.

"And I am Dean Amos Boyd, head of the boy's wing called Alaric. Also named after the founder of the boy's wing." He smiled at the boys.

"Everyone, please separate and follow your house, Dean, to your wing." Headmaster Louis tapped on the metal gates with his cane, and they opened wide.

Everyone split into groups and followed the Deans. The Florence Wing was to the right of the mansion, the Alaric Wing was to the left of the mansion, and the headmaster stood on the middle path to the mansion, smiling at us.

Once we reached the mansion, bright red and yellow double doors opened, and a fancy water fountain sat in the middle of the marble floor. Light brown doors lined the bright marble hallway, and little signs were hammered on the doors.

Across the hall was the common room, which was where the boys and girls could meet.

"Down there is the common room. That's where you can study, read a book, or hang out with friends! But, no boy is allowed in the girl's wing, and no girl is allowed in the boy's wing," Dean Beatrice stared blankly down the hall.

"There's also a staircase at the end of both hallways that leads to your classes and dining hall," Dean Beatrice said, pointing to a red-carpeted staircase at the end of the hallway.

"Rest time is at nine o'clock p.m., and bedtime is at nine-thirty p.m. The doors close to the common room at ten, but I expect NONE of you to leave your dormitories past nine-thirty. Is that clear?"

Everyone nodded their heads.

"I am going to take attendance and show you and your roommate to your dorm," Dean Beatrice smiled, walked in front of the double doors, and took attendance.

"Sadie McMillion and Alexandra Faith, room One," She smiled and pointed to room one.

The two girls seemed happy.

"Sage Caitlyn and Garcia Daniel, Room Two. You can find your uniforms in your dresser already, Sage," Beatrice grinned at me and pointed to the door in front of Alexandra and Sadie.

"Thank you," I smiled and opened the door to see a massive bedroom with two queen-sized beds with red pajamas lying on them and pillows with the initials of my first and last name.

There's a marble structure that makes up the whole room. At the end of the room was a door to the right, and two bean bags and a large white bookcase sat behind them.

In front of our beds were white dressers already filled with uniforms. "How lucky we are to get together, eh!" Garcia walked over to her dresser and dropped her duffel bag next to it.

"I know! This room is awesome!" I walked over to my bed after closing the door.

"That door down there is the bathroom, by the way." Garcia pointed to the brown door. "Okay, cool," I looked at my dresser and saw my schedule on top of it.

"Oh, so, I see here that I have math and English, but then I also have archery and LCP. What's that?" I look up from my paper and see Garcia sitting in the fluffy bean bag, reading one of the hundreds of books aligned along the walls.

"Oh! That's Learning to Control your Powers, very important," Garcia nodded and returned to reading.

"BONG! BONG! BONG!"

"Get your uniform on! It's time for orientation!" Garcia hopped up happily and threw her uniform on, so I did the same.

"Also, there is no changing room beside the loo, so I'll take it," Garcia rushed to the bathroom, holding her clothes.

"Oh, okay-" I opened my drawer and saw the same outfit Ezran was wearing, only a skirt instead of shorts. The shoes were even there.

"Okay, you ready?" Garcia walked out of the bathroom wearing the red uniform and fiery red eyeshadow.

"Yep!" I threw on a red watch and tied my shoes, and soon enough, we were walking out the door.

"Oof, what time is lunch?" I rubbed my stomach as I followed Garcia up the red stairs.

"Right now!" She said happily, running up the stairs.

"No running, Ms. Daniel," Beatrice followed behind me. "Sorry!" Garcia slowed to a stop and waited for me.

"Keep going, you two," Beatrice waved her hand up the stairs.

We walked to big wooden double doors, seeing rows of gray leather benches and white wood tables with food on each one.

One long table sat in front of the students' tables, which is where all of the teachers sat.

"Okay, over here," two blond girls ran past Garcia and me, giggling and latching arms.

"Let's sit over here," I made a beeline for wherever Ezran was. Even if we didn't sit *with* him. "But that's where Ezran is sitting-Ohhh,"

"Hm-hm-hm," Garcia shook her shoulders and smirked at me.

"Oh my gosh, you are *hilarious*. Haha". We laughed and walked over to a different table. "I think I should work up my confidence before I sit over there." Garcia agreed.

"Wow! Look at this amazing spread!" Garcia started piling potatoes and salad onto her plate. I just took some potatoes and a slice of honeyed ham.

After orientation, we had two hours to sit in the common room and hang out.

"So, is this gonna be every day? Sitting in the common room for two hours?" I asked as Garcia and I walked down the stairs.

"Yes, but it's at different times each day," Garcia said, sitting on a black leather couch.

"Like on Mondays, like today, the two hours is after lunch, and on Tuesdays, it's after your first study." She waved her hands around as she talked. More people filled the room while others returned to their dorms.

"Are people allowed to sleep during this time?" I asked, staring into a blazing stone fireplace. "Yep! This is kinda your free time, if you will," Garcia waved her hand again.

"I'm gonna get a cup of hot cocoa from the Dining Hall. Do you want anything?" She hopped up out of the chair and walked toward the stairs.

"I'll have a bowl of pretzels, please!" I said, stealing her chair. "On it!"

I pulled out a book from the shelves behind the sitting area and sat down again when I saw the boys rumble into the common room. Many of them were laughing about whatever food fight they got into last year.

"Oh, look who it is, the first year," Ezran emerged from the rabble.

"Why are you being so mean, like? What's the point?" I looked up from my book and uncrossed my legs to stare into Ezran's cold brown eyes.

Ezran sighed, laughed, and crouched down in my chair.

"Look, you will not survive here. LCP is the hardest class, and I know that is one of the classes you have this year, and let me tell you this," He sighed again and put up a finger.

"The kids with that class are deranged, demented, unstable, and incredibly mental! You won't last a minute there!" He smiled sarcastically and stood up to look down at me.

"Why don't you need it then," I crossed my arms and stood up.

"Well, I am not an overly sensitive maniac like you and can control what I do," Ezran held his hand in front of me and did a fingershake, and a butterfly appeared.

"How did you-" I reached out to his hand.

"Ah-Ah-ah, not until you tell me why you have that LCP class," He smirked and pulled back his hand.

I breathed in big, "When people say things that I don't like, my eyes turn green, and a green aura appears in my hands, and I can't control it," I sighed hard.

"Oh my god,"

"So you better watch it!" I went onto my tiptoes to try and look Ezran in the eyes to intimidate him, but instead, my feet lifted off the ground, and I was flying.

"SAGE!!" Garcia dropped white mugs full of steaming cocoa and raced down the stairs.

CHAPTER 6

Some force had taken hold of me and swept me off my feet. At first, I was not so aware of it. Panic struck the moment I realized that I couldn't feel the ground. To the same effect, I fell to the ground. Dean Beatrice and Amos Boyd came rushing from the teacher's lounge.

"Ah!" I heard someone gasp and shout, "She's a monster," in the distance, and I knew it was being directed at me. I wasn't even sure what was happening. Ezran paced back and forth, glancing at me with confusion and shock.

That was it. I had officially screwed up my chances of being considered one of the "*cool ones.*" It was my first day at this new school, and my reputation and sense of respect were on the line! We were hardly through the first class, and I had already managed to mess that up somehow". I got up slowly, trying to keep myself balanced. Ezran climbed the boy's stairs, cutting one last glance before vanishing.

"Sage, are you okay? What was that?" Everyone in the common room was staring at me.

"My power," I sighed and walked back to my dorm.

"Okay, people, nothing to worry about, Ms. Caitlyn here, okay. Your studies will start earlier today so you can meet your teachers," Beatrice said, walking toward the stairs. "Hey, Uhm, Sage," Garcia set a hand on my shoulder and walked with me to our dorm.

"Yes," I wiped tears off my cheeks quickly.

"I hope your classes go okay, and I'll see you at dinner," Garcia gave me a weak smile, and rushed ahead of me to get her bags.

"Thanks-" I sighed as I walked towards the stairs.

I saw that my first class was English and I had it with Ezran. I was excited and also very upset. After my blowout incident in the common room, I already don't want to be seen.

I walked and pushed open the shiny glass door and saw the only seat open, and coincidentally, that one was the one next to Ezran.

"Wow," I whispered disappointingly with my eyes affixed to the floor as I walked quickly to the desk.

"Well, hello there," Ezran sounded sympathetic.

"Hi," I cleared my throat and stared at the blackboard.

"Are you okay?" He shifted in his seat to look at me.

"Yes," I closed my eyes.

"Good," He sat up and copied my blank stare.

"Oh look, the teachers here!" An old man walked into the room and started talking about nouns and verbs. I opened my notebook and wrote down things I needed to study when Ezran caught my eye when he fixed his fluffy hair.

"Class, I need you to pay attention. Headmaster Louis would like to put on two dances this year. One for the beginning of the year and another at the end of the year." Spit flew from the teacher's mouth as he yelled across the room.

After the barking announcement, all the girls in the classroom turned their heads to look over at Ezran and me.

"Girls, let's all focus on our studies and worry about the ball later," The teacher let out a raspy chuckle and continued talking.

* * *

"What class do you have next?" Garcia met me outside of the English room.

"OOH! Class with Ezran, how'd that go?" She laughed, and we started to walk. Ezran hurried in front of me to his next class.

"I- fine?" I continued to walk to math.

"Oh, here's my class. I'll see ya later." I waved to her as I stepped into the classroom, only to find that all the kids had gone *haywire.*

"Okay, kids, settle down," the sweet voice of a younger woman echoed. She sat at a worn wooden desk and looked up at the wild class with her piercing glance.

Kids were running around, yelling and throwing paper airplanes. I could see the teacher was struggling, and it was kinda funny.

After around two hours of math, it was finally time for dinner. I stood up off of my seat, practically peeling my thighs off the blue plastic chair and headed toward the staircase. Two boys bumped into me. They looked back and glared at me. "What the heck was all that about? Maybe Ezran said something to them? I whispered to myself, glaring back at them bravely. I wasn't sure why my first day had become the worst day, let alone everyone acting like I was a menace to society or something..."

"OUCH! WHAT THE HECK!" I squealed.

"Freak," A long blond haired girl ran into me on the stairs, dropping her books, her dark red eyes scorned at me. It would be after a few seconds that, she would scream, which sounded more like an animal screeching in agony. Then, she vanished into the dark corners of the shadows.

"Did a ghost just yell at me?" I was puzzled...

Who is that? What just happened? Where is Garcia? And why is everything so weird? I wondered, making my way through the common room. About halfway through, I noticed a strange black fog-like material quickly forming on the floor of the room and from it, Ezran emerged.

"Ezran?" I stood in utter shock, standing stiff and blinking, frozen for a few microseconds, maybe...

"Did you make all the people hate me? What was that?" Ezran walked slowly toward me.

Did you have anything to do with this?" I let my shoulders relax, and my blood flowed back into my toes.

"Actually, yes, yes I do," The fog finally dissipated, and Ezran stood right before me.

"All of this is a vision," Ezran waved his hands around.

"It's not real." Ezran continued to explain.

What the heck did he mean by "it's not real"... I pondered. After seeing all the weird stuff I've seen so far on my first day at School, I don't think anything could surprise me anymore.

"I ended up passing out on the grass, using up every bit of my strength to create this...simulation for you." Ezran gestured around, proud of his childish play. He held out his hand for me to reach, and so I did.

"So, uh-what- am I real?" I pulled my hand back.

"Well, no-" I cut Ezran off with another question.

"And why were you so mean to me at the beginning of school?"

My view began to spin in an unnatural way. I wasn't really sure if it was my head messing with me or if it was the illusion that Ezran claimed that he had done it, but one thing was for sure, something wasn't right. The spinning increased, and Ezran had blurred out of my sight. Shortly after, I found myself sprawling down, fading into some other place. I suddenly woke, jerking upward, and noticed the bright sun peering over me. Then, I saw my math teacher hovering over my desk. Although I felt fine, I did feel a slight difference in my breathing. "Did I just teleport?" I thought to myself.

"Miss Caitlyn, you were expected at dinner five minutes ago, wash up at once!"

"Yes, Ma'am!" I quickly hopped off my seat, rushed to gather my things, and dashed out the door. Ezran seemed to be in a rush, too.

"What are you doing here? I need NO distractions right now," I whispered and skipped quickly in front of him. "I want to talk about the vision," he said. He stumbled behind me and fell to the marble floor.

"Ezran, are you okay?" I didn't want to be too empathetic since I barely knew him.

"I TOLD YOU, I USED ALL OF MY STRENGTH TO CREATE THAT VISION FOR YOU!"

"AND YOU HAD TO RUIN IT BY ASKING QUESTIONS!" Ezran yelled at me as he sat up.

"Oh- uh-" Whatever that means, I thought to myself. I didn't have anything left to say. I got up off my knees and rushed to the dining hall, his words ringing in my ears.

CHAPTER 7

Afew weeks later, my first learning to control powers class started. The room is dark and cold. Small rooms lined along a dark and long hallway. The sight was creepy, I silently thought to myself. The rooms have names written in chalk on a blackboard beside a soundproof metal door.

All seven kids stood in an anxious cluster in the middle of the hallway, blathering nervously. A tall, old gray man in a black five-piece suit holding seven straight jackets politely walked toward the cluster.

"My name is Sir Alfred Benedict. I am the LCP dean. I don't teach, I watch, I don't help, I just observe."

"Now, I expect you to find your rooms quietly and quickly. There are soundproof doors, screaming will not be heard, and anything that may affect other people shall not work. Guards stand by every door. They will let you in and out. As I said, you will not be heard, so I get to decide how long your rooms will remain locked. You will be released once you have finished your training, even if it takes ten hours! You will be fed through a small slot that's on your doors. You will sleep on the floor. Undergarments will be provided at midnight. Good luck." He gave us a toothy smile and turned away to watch the kids walk down the ill-lit hallway. When I found my way to my door, a strong guard shoved me into the room. He quickly slammed the door behind me as if I was going to make an attempt to make a run for it.

I quickly noticed how small and tight the space was. The walls and floor were aligned with padding that lined the room. It was like a dungeon, only slightly luxurious and nothing else besides the silence. The door had a small window in the middle. I walked back to sit on the soft ground when something caught my attention from the corner of my eye.

"Wow, where did you come from?" I whispered. It was a brightly blue colored-purple dotted butterfly. I stretched a finger out, and it landed on it perfectly. I tried to pet it, and it started talking.

"Ah! Finally! I can talk!" The voice was familiar.

"Wha-wait. Garcia, is that you?" I held the butterfly close to my ear, hoping that I could make out what it said.

"Yes, it is." I flew into your room before the guard closed the door.

"But how?" I was confused.

"I shapeshifted secretly behind Sir- whatever his name was..." Garcia grinned widely so that I could see it on her small face.

"But you're not supposed to be in here. I will probably go mad, like all of the other kids. I'm gonna be here for ten hours!" I curse under my breath and flop over to the padded floor.

"Well then, I guess I'll just have to fly out. Oh wait, I can't." Garcia remembered.

Suddenly, Gacia transformed into a growling tiger, piercing her gaze straight through me.

"Garcia, fight it, don't do this!" I panicked and quickly ran to the other side of the room.

"Oh-h-h, but I can't." She said in a gruff voice. She slowly walked towards me, swaying her head and biting into the air.

"AAHHHH!" a loud echoing scream bounced off the walls while my room lit up brightly with a green aura.

The feline, too, seemed startled by the sudden change. I was in the air in seconds, perhaps even higher than the ceiling itself. Somehow, I may have just gone through the roof. I looked down to see Garcia and saw a strange transformation happening to her. Her skin changed to light green, then solid green, and into powdery form. It was like a million tiny green embers falling from her all at once, obliviating into a small pile of glittery nothingness. I fall onto it like a cloth, closing my eyes gently and drifting into sleep.

"Geeze, I had a crazy dream." I sat up and looked around. Half expecting to be in my soft bed in my dormitory. But instead, I was still in the soundproof padded room in the mansion's basement.

I realized this wasn't a dream when I saw a pile in the dark corner of the room. Just like the visions, I saw if it was a dream. But if it was a dream, how could it be a reality?

"Oh god, oh, god, OH GOD!! The dream was real. Wait, what about Garcia? Does she have powers?! How did she get in? And my most confusing question was why she would want to hurt me?! AHH!" I screamed again, and tears streamed down my face in utter confusion, which made a small puddle beneath me. I laid back down next to the pile of dust. It twinkled like gems, even though it was dark in the room. This pile of dust was once Garcia. I cried silently until a gray hand opened a small slot in my door. He slid a plate of greens, potatoes and a thin slice of meat that looked like turkey.

"Thanksgiving for naughty children is...lovely," A familiar male voice said from a dark, fog-filled corner of my room. He held the same plate I did. Full of food.

"Uhm, sure," I get up off my knees and walk over to the corner to sit beside the mystery boy. "Let's eat shall we?" He shuffled in front of me with his head down and eventually raised his head to reveal his eyes.

"Ezran?" He sat in front of me, his hair nicely combed and a dead daisy in his blazer pocket.

"Eat," He said, jabbing his fork into his hand. Blood trickled down his boney fingers and onto the floor.

"Ezran? Why are you acting like this?" I grasp my plate tightly in case I have to throw it.

"I said EAT!" Ezran flew close to my face and yelled loudly. I turned my face away, and he huffed loudly in my ear.

After his 5-second splurge moment, he sat down gently and smiled cheerfully.

I quickly picked up my fork and butter knife and rapidly diced the green beans. Due to the madness in my hand motion, it slipped, and the knife's edge grazed against my knee.

"Ah, it's deep," it hurts, but I didn't show it.

Trying my best to avoid Ezran noticing the stream of blood slipping down my knee somehow, but he catches on quickly. Ezran leaps forward to cover my knee with his blood-soaked hands. The burning sensation increases. It was like someone had sprinkled salt on the wound.

"AH! Ezran! Take your hand off of me!" I tried to stand, but Ezran's other hand grabbed my shoulder and pushed me down to the floor.

Ezran peers down at me with a smile. A haunting, crazed-wicked smile. I knew right then that he was going to do something. His creepy smile said it all.

I strained with all my might to awaken, fire up, charge, or do whatever I needed to get my power working. But nothing happened. I gave up when I realized that I was just holding my breath the whole time. I had no idea what I was doing, really.

"Give up. You are weak. Your powers are weak. Weak people don't get to wield any power. Your powers will not work," Ezran laughed and applied more pressure to my wounded knee.

""GET OFF OF ME!!" I flushed in anger as the pain in my knee became too much of an agony. At that very moment, I felt it. I felt my energy levels suddenly rising and could now wield the power. The power to kick him straight in the face. Which only made things worse.

I gathered my energy and went for the kill. I kicked him so hard that he flew to the other side of the room. In the distance, I watched him get up, dust off the debris and hold tight to his "gushing fountain of blood" nose.

"We're doing this. Okay. My turn," He slowly walked over to me. He comes close enough that we see eye to eye. He takes his hand and slowly brings it to his temple. I couldn't back away, it was like I was stuck in some trance.

"Ezran, please, don't do this, please." Tears streamed down my face.

His hand swiftly guts me in the stomach. I clutched my stomach and coughed up a few bloody spits.

I felt the power rise inside me again, and without thinking, I quickly sprinted forward and charged with a tight fist. I swung as hard as I could and thudded loudly on contact.

He stood strangely stiff. It's as if he turned himself into stone.

The blood stains on his clothes began to dissipate and fade. The blood on the floor, too, began to fade. I looked down at my knee. The gash was still a nasty, bloody site. I looked back up and saw the ghostly figure of Ezran before vanishing.

CHAPTER 8

I wasn't sure what I was supposed to do in this "dungeon" or how I was supposed to pass this test. Unfortunately, they didn't give us an instructional guide. I wasn't even sure how this dungeon would help me control my powers. I stood before the fading Ezran long before hearing what sounded like footsteps. After a short pause, I could hear the sounds of the door's mechanism turning. The doors swung open, and a guard stood before me, handing me a bottle of water and a towel.

"Congrats, Sage, you've passed!" The guard shook my hand gracefully and smiled. I step outside of the dungeon, feeling relieved. The lights around us made it hard for me to keep my eyes open, but I knew they would adjust after a while.

"Good job, Miss Caitlyn. Your test is now over," Sir Alfred Benedict walked over with a cheery smile. He stretched his hand out. Although my hands were smeared in blood, I still shook his hand.

"Please allow me to explain further. You see, Miss Caitlyn, although what you witnessed was terrifying, I can assure you that they were just illusions, tailored specifically to test your fear and how you operate under pressure. We considered putting the people you cared for the most in that room with you. Sure, we could have used our imagination and placed more common beasts or enemies, but that wouldn't help you tap into your true essence. Something about "love" tends to bring out the best versions of us," Sir Alfred Benedict cheerfully explained while I still stood in a trance of trauma.

People that I loved? I love my mother. I love Ivy. But I did not see them during the test.

Perhaps Sir Alfred Benedict was right. If the illusions had shown me my closest family members, perhaps I wouldn't have been able to see through it. Maybe I wouldn't be able to use my powers. Sir Alfred Benedict's explanation was sound, and it brought me comfort to know that it wasn't real. At least for now, it wasn't.

"Now you can go upstairs and wash up and rest. Everyone has the day off, so go see your friends." Sir Alfred pointed his gray boney finger toward the stairs.

I quickly went up the staircase, my bottle of water in one hand and the towel hoisted under my arm. The first person I saw was Ezran. His hair was combed, and a daisy in his pocket. The first thought that crept into my mind was, *was he real?*

"Ezran, a-a-are you r-r-real?" I nervously questioned my vision. "Yes, I'm real," He smiled at me and not the kind of madman's smile the fake Ezran had.

"Let's go down to the common room." Ezran reached his hand out.

I playfully slapped his hand, "Not before I take a hot shower!"

He scanned me with his eyes and noticed the blood from my knee wound.

"Yes, nothings better than a nice bath. I'll wait here." Ezran pulled out the same book he was reading on the bus and crossed his legs when I saw bloody scratch marks.

I immersed myself in the hot shower that felt like heaven. I looked down at the drain and saw dark red stringy-filament patterns mixed with water that formed a whirlpool. I hadn't noticed how much blood was lost until I had washed the stains from my knee wound and around my leg. It made me wonder if it was going to leave a scar.

I quickly dressed, brushed my hair to perfection, and jolted back down to Ezran.

When I arrived, Ezran looked the same. His hair was neatly combed, and he had a gentle smile that only brightened up when our eyes met.

"Hot Cocoa?" Ezran gently waved a steamy cup head-high.

"Just what I needed," I took the cup from him. The cup's warmth was soothing, so I held it closer to my chest as we walked.

"Come, sit right here," Ezran patted the leather chair on which Garcia sat a few weeks ago.

I was still in somewhat of a trauma, unable to talk correctly. But I tried anyway.

"O-o-okay," I carefully sat down.

A few seniors walked by and made remarks, "Hey, new girl, we've all been through it. Don't be so hard on yourself," Ezran's eyes pierced theirs, which quickly silenced them. They humbly went about their day, and Ezran turned his attention towards me.

"You know, those guys over there are right. We all know what it's like being in that... *box*." It's the most terrible thing that anyone can go through, but at the same time, it is the most important phase of your training. I know it's tough right now to process this, but in time, you will see why the lock-up was mandatory. Only time can tell", Ezran explained as his eyes were fixed on mine. I could tell he had so much more he wanted to share with me. But he kept that part silenced, and perhaps it was done for a good reason. Yet another mystery that only time could tell.

"You want to talk about the-" Ezran searched my eyes.

"Learning t-t-to control p-p-powers, not e-easy," I took small sips. "I got badly h-hurt", Ezran glanced at the gash on my knee. I tried my best not to stutter.

"I remember my first time in the chamber. You passed your test pretty quickly as compared to others. Some, like me, spent weeks in there," Ezran's voice humbled.

His confession relieved me, and I felt somewhat empowered. I would recover from this and improve my ability to control my powers.

We both stared into the fireplace, allowing shared horrors to sync. I watched the fire dance in a rhythm as if the fire was moving to some music. A small smile formed, and Ezran quickly noticed. He searched my eyes, looking for clues as to why I smiled.

"So, when exactly is the dance?" I nervously asked.

"The dance? Oh, the daaance! Yes. Thanks for reminding me. I nearly had forgotten about that. So, yes, it's tomorrow night, " Ezran stood in front of me, took the hot cup, and placed it on the side table.

"Stand up," Ezran commanded, and I obeyed immediately.

I stood up, and we met eye to eye. I was nervous. I wasn't sure where this was going, but I liked it.

"So, I know I've been really mean to you and all, and I acted like that because I think you're beautiful."

A brief, awkward silence filled the air between us. I didn't know what to say.

"I've kinda been wanting to ask you something. You wanna go to the dance with me?" Ezran held his hand up. A faint glow illuminated his hands as he opened his palm, revealing a blooming red rose that opened before me.

I cupped the beautiful fiery rose from his palm and brought it close to the tip of my nose. "Smells good, doesn't it?" Ezran softly laughed and shook his hand.

"Yes." I cupped the beauty close to me. The fragrance was vibrant but also pleasant.

"So...yes, you are going to the dance, or yes, the flower smells good?" Ezran's tone was humorous and charming. This was a side of Ezran that I hadn't seen before.

"Yes to both," I returned the reply with a smile.

"This is such a beautiful rose, Ezran," I eyed the beauty up close.

"It reminded me of you," he said, gazing into my eyes.

Out of the corner of my eye, I saw Garcia walking down the stairs, gripping tightly to the railing with blood dripping down her forehead.

"Excuse me one second, Ezran," I took my attention away from his charming self and focused on the blood-drenched Garcia.

"LCP nearly killed me," Garcia's voice was frantic.

"I thought I could handle it since I've had it twice in the two years I've been here, this was so, so much worse," Garcia grabbed a hold of my forearm and slid past Ezran to sit in the worn black leather chair.

"It's okay, just breathe," I knelt next to her and held her pale hand.

"Think of butterflies and rainbows, no, never mind, no butterflies," I remembered what happened in the mansion's basement.

"Oh! I know what will cheer you up!" I snapped out of my flashback and turned my focus toward Garcia.

"What?"

"Ezran asked me to the dance tonight!" I jump up and squeal. Garcia seemed unfazed by my excitement. She stared blankly into the blazing fire.

"Oh really! That's awesome!" Garcia turned her head back to me and got almost just as excited.

"I wish someone would ask me to the dance," Garcia looked down sadly. "Well, is there anyone here you want to go with?" I asked sympathetically. "Well, yes, there is." Garcia blushed furiously.

"Who, who!!" I got so excited.

"His name is Ajax. He's super nice," Garcia said, his face turning tomato red.

"What's his power?" Ezran politely watched us mingle.

"Well, we never really talked much, but there was definitely eye chemistry. I am actively preparing so many questions for him. All I know is that he is a werewolf and a really amazing artist."

"What does Ajax look like?"

"Dreamy. He's tall, slim and has dirty blonde hair, but he makes it look sooo cool."

I noticed a figure descending the stairs. His eyes fixed on Garcia.

"We would glance at each other from time to time, you know," Garcia didn't notice Sage's gaze shift towards the unknown-handsome figure.

"Hum, Garcia. I think your 'Prince Charming' just arrived", I gestured her towards the direction of the stairs. My words interrupted her, and she sharply stopped.

"Huh? Where?

Garcia turned and saw Ajax. He stood just as Garcia recalled. Slim and dirty blonde hair. He held a large bouquet of white roses and daisies and quickly hid it behind him as if Garcia hadn't noticed. He walked right up to the three of us. Oddly, he didn't say a word, so I had to break the ice for them.

"So, you're Ajax? I present myself in the nicest way possible.

"Yes, I am! And you are?" He bowed to greet me.

"Oh, I'm Sage, originally from New York City, but then I moved here."

"Oh! You're from Earth as well! I happen to be from Edinburgh, Scotland!" He crossed his legs and leaned against the wall.

"I could tell by your accent-"

"EHEM," Garcia got impatient, nudging me with her elbow.

"Hi A-ajax!" She eagerly jumped up and stood upright, facing Ajax.

"Well, uhm, Garcia, I wanted to ask you something," he said, attempting to hide the oversized bouquet behind his back.

"Will you go to the dance with me?" Garcia blurted, her face burning.

"You beat me to it," Ajax said, grinning.

"Yeah, I guess I did." Ajax held out the bouquet to Garcia, who took it gently.

CHAPTER 9

"Garcia! I didn't pack any dresses!" I flutter my hands in front of my face in panic, pacing back and forth by my dresser.

"It's okay, neither did I," she gritted her teeth, clenched her fists, and looked up from her dresser drawer.

"Knock, Knock," Dean Beatrice walked into our room wearing a lavender purple dinner dress.

"Girls, I heard that you two didn't have dresses! Well, no problem tonight, the school gave all the girls a little money that you can spend on dresses and accessories for this wonderful evening!"

"The school bus will be leaving around four thirty p.m." Dean Beatrice smiled softly and walked out of our room.

"Oh my, the bus leaves in five! We got to go!" Garcia glanced at her watch and pulled me out of the room.

"Wait! My shoes!" I ran back to our dorm, slipping on the marble floor to grab my buckle shoes. I look at myself quickly in the mirror and pull down on my sweater vest.

"Come on, slowpoke! I don't want to miss the bus!" Garcia slid into the room and dragged me away from the mirror.

We walked down the path, seeing many blue buses that lined the gates.

"ALL ABOARD! SIR THEODORE SCHOOL TO LUCIFER CENTER!" a British man cupped his hand and yelled to the kids streaming from the doors.

Garcia climbed on the bus, but the man placed a hand on my shoulder and stopped me.

"Hey!" My voice directed to the man, and he smirked back at me.

"Don't get on this bus," he said wryly.

"But my friend is on this bus!" I squirmed my shoulders to try and catch the bus. The engines turned over, and dark smoke started to puff.

"NO!" I squirmed and kicked when I saw Ezran running toward the man holding me. "Let her go, you-" Ezran cussed at the man and held his hand in front of the man's face.

The man gargled and choked as he clenched his throat.

"Please- let me- go, I'll let- your friend- on the- bus!" The man struggled to breathe as he fell to the ground.

"Why did you stop me anyway?" I look at the top of the man's sweaty, bald head.

"No time to chat, get on!" Ezran yanked me toward the bus and threw me on the steppes as he followed behind me.

I went to sit with Garcia, but she had apparently got a seat with Ajax.

I sat in an empty seat behind Garcia and Ajax, not expecting Ezran to join me.

"Oh hey, you don't have to sit with me," I moved closer to the window as Ezran slid into the seat. We jolted forward as the bus started to move.

"Too late now," He smiled at me and waved a book into his hand.

He crossed his legs and opened the book that emerged from his palm. But he quickly set it down and turned to face me. I look over at him.

"Do you know who that person is?" Ezran cocked his head to the side. "No, not at all," I said in return.

"Well, that's kinda creepy for that random guy just to stop you randomly." "Yeah," I looked out the window as many trees and grasslands zoomed by.

We sat in silence, I looked out the window, and Ezran read his book. A booming voice over a loudspeaker said, "Sir Theodore School to Lucifer Center!" The bus stopped quickly by a cobblestone sidewalk.

As I got off the bus, I met up with Garcia, who was still stuck in Ajax. Ezran ran off to a group of boys. They all waved at me and started walking toward a men's apparel store. I looked in front of me and saw an antique clothing store.

"Antique clothing?" I walked up to the door and pushed it. Small bells rang above me, and a massive whiff of old punched me in the face, causing me to sneeze. I looked around and saw many unique ball gowns and dinner dresses. A small woman peeked out of the front counter, and I saw it was my mom!

"Mom?" I said excitedly. I ran up to her but stopped abruptly, realizing I knew nothing about her except that she was my mom.

"Hey! Parents are allowed to come to Lucifer Center today, and I wanted to check on you! How's my little baby doing?" Mom grabbed my hands. I let her hold them, but it was weird, being that I remember nothing of her.

"So, this place is interesting," I look around and start pacing the dress racks.

"Hah, yeah, but I know you'd like it, so I decided to greet you here!" Mom started to pace with me.

"So, are you enjoying school? What classes are you taking?" Mom pulled out a sapphire blue dress from the sixties.

"I am taking all sorts of classes. The first couple of weeks were just regular school stuff. We did math and English. Then we were going to do archery and horseback riding and art and just about anything fancy after that," I looked at the ceiling, which had many cobwebs and dust on it.

"Did anyone ask you to the dance?" Mom looked stern. Almost like she didn't want me to go.

I hesitated to tell her the most popular guy asked me out.

"Well, this kid named Ezran," I blushed and looked at my feet.

"Oh my! Is he cute?" Mom smiled and scratched her dirty blond hair. "Er..yeah."

"And really sweet," I paused.

"Who's really sweet?" Garcia walked into the building, still holding Ajax's arm. He looked uncomfortable. He shot me an uncomfortable smile.

"Oh, I was just telling my mom about Ezran "

"Mom, this is Garcia and Ajax," I did jazz hands to introduce them.

"Oh! Nice to meet you," Mom held her hand out to shake their hands. "You too!" Garcia grinned at my mom.

"So, you need some help finding an outfit!" Garcia finally let go of Ajax and jumped up and down with excitement.

54

"Sure!" Garcia took my hand and raced by Mom to a rack full of purple dresses. "This one's cute!" Garcia pulled out a hideous fuchsia dress from the seventies.

"Haha, maybe for my grandma!" I pulled out a beautiful sage green floral prom dress. "Woah," Garcia walked over to me with her mouth gaping.

"This, this is it!" I hold up the dress over my head and race to the counter. "This is a really cute dress, Sage!" Mom took my dress and scanned the tag.

"Ooh, this dress was brought in yesterday!" Mom said excitedly as she looked at the paper tag.

Mom put the dress in a paper bag and gave me a goodbye hug.

Garcia and I stepped out of the store and saw the buses were getting ready to leave.

"Oh shoot!" Garcia and I race to get on the bus. We got on just quick enough to sit down together.

"Whew," Garcia let out a long sigh as she hugged her dress bag. "What dress did you get?" I look at her with soft eyes.

"A pink short tea dress. It's a pretty simple gown." Garcia pulled a bit of the fabric out of the brown paper bag.

"Oh, pretty!" I rubbed the small patch of fabric, and Garcia stuffed it back in the bag.

"So tell me about Ajax! Like, I know he's a werewolf, but tell me about him," I press my elbows into my thigh and rest my chin on my knuckles.

"Well, he's sweet, supportive, protective of me, a great dancer and artist, but he could leave you in a pool of your blood if you got on his nerves," Garcia turned a shade of scarlet.

"Woah! No need to get that graphic!" I pat her on the back. Garcia chuckled and relaxed a bit.

"Oh, look! It's Ajax's field!" she pointed a bony finger before my face. I looked over abruptly and saw the most beautiful meadow I'd ever laid my eyes on. Bright green grass sprung up happily from the ground while many beautiful and colorful flowers hugged the grass. The wind softly blew, making the grass and flowers sway like a slow dance.

"And that's his painting rock right there, by the creek and the weeping willow," Garcia took my head and positioned it where I could see a massive weeping willow tree sitting perfectly over a smooth stone that posed by a softly running creek.

"He's got it going on! With his paint studio, I mean," I turn back to Garcia after gazing at the wonder.

"I know, right? I want him to ask me out and take me there, just to sit, talk about life, maybe have a picnic," Garcia sighed contently. And slumped in her part of the leather bus seat.

—— Chapter 10 ——

After Garcia and I arrived back at the mansion, we were in the process of getting ready when we were startled by a knock on the door.

"Wonder who that is," I brushed down my skirt in case it was Ezran, which it was.

"Oh, hi, Ezran! I thought boys couldn't come over," I cocked my head to the side as I pressed my shoulder into my brown door.

" There was an excuse tonight." Ezran grinned softly.

"Oh, well," I looked behind me to ensure Garcia was ready. "Come in!" I open the door wider, and Ezran walks in politely.

"Ezran, do you have any idea where Ajax is? He hasn't said a word to me since we were at Lucifer Center." Garcia pulled on the bottom half of her pink skirt, looking confused. "I mean, no, the last time I saw him was when you two visited Sage in the dress store," Ezran looked concerned.

We stood around for a few awkward minutes when the ground started to shake badly.

"Ah! Is there an earthquake or something!?" I fell to my knees and stomach, covering my neck and the lower portion of the back of my head with my hands.

"What the heck is an earthquake?" Ezran followed my move when the second rumble came.

"Sorry, otherworldly things," I breathe deeply, and a green aura appears in my hands. "Sage, you're flying again," Garcia looked up from her cocoon on the floor.

"Oh really! You think I don't know that?" I kick my legs, hoping that I will float down. My neck jerked back, and I fell to the floor.

"Sage, are you okay?" Ezran got up from his cocoon and tugged on my shoulders to sit me straight up.

"Yeah, that was weird. It was like something that wasn't supposed to be here started to take control of me," I shivered as Ezran helped me up. I brushed my shoulders and looked up at the ceiling.

"I'm just curious, can you fly at will?" Garcia looked intrigued. Like I was some kind of bird.

"I'll try," I looked up at the ceiling and clenched my fists, but nothing happened. "Guess not."

"Oh," she looked disappointed. Garcia looked at her watch and quickly hopped off her bed.

"What's the rush?" I look up at her.

"It's time for the dance!" Garcia had tears in her eyes.

"Oh!" Ezran stood up quickly and helped me up from the floor.

"Garcia, what's wrong?" Ezran and I stop before we head out the door. "Ajax isn't here," She looked down at her dress.

"Maybe he's meeting you upstairs?" I try to be positive.

"But we have to go. Sorry, Garcia," I shot her a sympathetic look, and Ezran and I walked out the door.

Ezran and I arrive at the dance. I scan the room for any sign of Ajax. Nothing.

"Welcome to the dance! I expect everyone had a good time at Lucifer Center?" The headmaster said from a microphone. The crowd screamed bloody murder like they were at some AC-DC concert.

"Okay, let's dance the night away!" The headmaster put the microphone down and turned on corny pop music.

The crowd danced happily, but I got a strange feeling in my stomach. I didn't want to start flying and look like I was possessed at the beginning of the dance.

Ezran noticed my nervous face. He took my hands, swung me around, and dipped me. "Woah!" I jerk up fast and look at Ezran shockingly.

"Where did you learn that!" I laugh.

"A little something I learned. You're so worried and sad all the time, so I wanted you to have some fun!"

"Well then!" I laughed a bit.

Garcia walked through the open double doors. She had a concerned and worried face. She scanned the room. I could tell by her face that there was no sign of Ajax. I saw Garcia sitting down at a table, and I decided to go over there.

"Garcia, are you okay?" I knelt beside her.

"No! I am not okay!" Garcia twirled her pink skirt, and tears made small splotches on her dress.

"Is there anything we can do, like get you to punch or something?"

"NO, Sage! NO! Punch doesn't fix anything! I was stupid enough to let him invite me to the dance! I knew he was going to leave me here! I should have never come to the dance!"

Garcia raced out of her seat and ran back to our dorm.

"Hmm, she's not feeling well," Ezran tried to lighten the mood. "Bad time," I patted his shoulder and gave him a sad smile.

Ezran and I walk back to the dance floor. Ezran brought me close to a window where the moonlight spilled its pale, bright light. I looked down at my feet, trying to hide my blushing face.

When I realized, my feet started to shake along with Ezran's hands. The window shattered before us, drowning out the laughter and music.

People screamed and hid under the tables. I looked above me, and the beautiful antique glass chandelier had come off its hinges. I raced out of the way. A hard clash of glass smacked against the ground, and shards flew everywhere. Soon enough, a massive gray tail whipped through the concrete walls. The beast emerged through the hole it made in the wall. It looked up and wailed loudly. I raced to the opposite side of the room and fired up my powers.

"OH, MY GOD! WHAT IS THAT!" Ezran shouted up at me as I flew up to the ceiling.

"IT'S A WYVERN! THE WORSE SPECIES OF DRAGONS!" I yell back down at him.

"GET UNDER A TABLE!" Ezran ran under a white cloth table, just like I said.

I flew over to the wyvern's face and pushed it with my power, but nothing happened. It started to huff, and soon, fire blazed out of its mouth. I move away quickly, but not quick enough for its tail not to hit me. I fell into a small corner of the room. The room spun as my eyes opened and closed tiredly.

The wyvern came close to my face and grabbed me by my dress. Its massive claws dug into my chest, causing me to bleed. I felt the heat and power surging through its bloodshot eyes.

I lay in its claws helplessly, contemplating why this is happening.

The pain of the wyvern's claws caused me to focus only on that instead of figuring out a plan to escape from this misery. I looked to the side and saw Garica slowly emerging into a fiery red wyvern.

She screeched and whipped her tail to hit the wyvern that held me in its grasp. It wailed as its claws slipped out of me. I fell to the ground but landed in welcoming arms instead of the cold concrete floor. Ezran held me tight and brought me out near Ajax's meadow. Ezran took off his blazer and wrapped it tightly around my chest to slow the bleeding. I looked at his once black blazer, which was now a dark red. I saw Ezran pace next to me, trying to figure out what to do. He muttered words that I could not comprehend. I felt strange and tingly as I saw my wounds slowly emerge back to normal. I sit up, and the pain has left me almost completely. I stand up slowly, and Ezran darts toward me. He wrapped his cold arms around me, warming us both up. My head sunk into his shoulder when something caught my eye. A body lay in the field not too far from Ezran and me. I looked behind me and saw Garcia was still fighting the wyvern.

"Oh, Garcia, I wanna help you," I softly whispered as Ezran grabbed my arm. "You okay?"

"Yeah, I'm fine, let's go see who that is," I held Ezran's hand nervously as we walked over to the body. I heard water ripples and soft leaves swaying together. I looked up and saw that we were at Ajax's meadow.

"Oh my god!" I looked at Ezran with my other hand cupped over my mouth. "What! Are you hurt!" Ezran squeezed my hand tighter.

"No! Worse! We're in Ajax's meadow!" I slowly looked down to my feet to see Ajax lying nearly dead in a small puddle of his blood.

"Oh my god!" Ezran's hand slipped out of mine as I started circling Ajax's body.

I carefully examined him, I noticed his painting apron was burnt at the hem, his pants were torn and ripped, I saw that his knees had been scratched and bloody, and his face was scraped and gashed.

"Help me get Ajax to the hospital wing," I said, kneeling to pick the upper half of his body out of the grass.

Ezran got a hold of Ajax's legs and heaved them over his shoulder. I walked close to Ezran, so Ajax's stomach sat on my shoulder.

"You can let his legs go now Ezran," I grunted, and his legs slammed into my knee.

"Are you okay? Do you need me to do anything? I mean, you did just recover from a dragon's claws that gashed into you."

"Nope, fine Ezran, thanks," The aura appeared, and my feet levitated only an inch off the ground. I groaned and jumped up but landed back on the grass.

"Dang it," I huff and keep walking toward the school.

Chapter 11

Once Ezran and I passed the tragedy of the once-perfect dining hall, we reached the hospital Wing.

"Here, I'll take Ajax, you go check on Garcia."

"Okay!" I gave Ezran a hug. Ajax groaned.

I darted back along the mansion, trying to find my way to the dining hall. I finally reached the steps that led to the common room.

Once I reached the big double doors, both of the wyverns lay on the floor helplessly.

"Garcia!!" I run over to the red wyvern. She wheezed as she breathed. I put my hand on her snout. She was very tired. I look over at the other wyvern that came to attack me. It looked defeated. I saw scratch marks all over its body. Some dried blood stain spots as well. I walked in front of its massive face. It breathed heavily as its eyes shut and opened tiredly. I set my hand on its wounds, and it deflated into heavy gray dust. It took the shape of the wyvern that was once lying before me. The dust blew away out into the night sky.

I ran over to Garcia, speaking softly to her.

"Garcia, there's something you must see," I said softly. "You need to change back," my breath trembled.

I stepped back as a breeze came between her and me. She slowly emerged back into a human.

First, her legs, then her head, and soon, she was lying in a small puddle of blood. She woke up and rubbed her face.

"Sage?" She whispered hoarsely.

"Garcia! You're awake!" I kneeled next to her.

"I need to take you to the hospital," I carefully put my hands under her back and knees. I pick her up slowly. She groaned as we started to walk.

"It's okay, we'll be there soon," my breath shakes under the weight.

We reached the hospital wing, seeing only Ajax lying in a bed. I saw Ezan sitting next to him in a chair, sleeping.

"Miss Ernestine! We have Garcia Daniel. She's badly hurt." I walk over to the bed next to Ajax and slowly set Garcia down. She flopped onto the bed tiredly and soon started to snore.

I plop down in the chair in between Garcia and Ajax. I rest my head on my knuckles and slowly drift off to sleep.

* * *

The next morning, I woke up to the warming sun and someone tapping my shoulder. "Sage, sage, wake up," I opened my eyes and saw it was Garcia.

"Hey, sleepy," she giggled as she shifted in her bed. "Hey," I rubbed my eyes.

"Why are you up? Shouldn't you be resting?" I asked, stretching my legs out.

"Yeah, I can't walk for at least a month or shapeshift," She flipped the covers off her legs, and I saw stitches everywhere.

"They stitched me up while I was sleeping. When I woke up, Ms. Ernestine said I couldn't walk for a while." Garcia traced out one of the scars on her legs.

"Oh my, I'm so sorry," I leaned in for a hug. Garcia winced as I touched her back.

"Have you seen who else is here?" I pulled open a curtain that separated Garcia and Ajax. "Ajax!" Garcia jumped off the bed.

"Garcia!" I caught her before she fell to the ground.

"Now, Miss Daniel, he's still unconscious." Ms. Ernestine appeared out of nowhere. "Oh, when will he not be?" I pushed Garcia back up to her bed.

"Maybe a little after lunch," The nurse brought pills in a paper cup and set it on Ajax's nightstand.

"Oh," Garcia looked down at her sheets.

"Sage, I'm gonna have to escort you and Ezran out so we can give our patients some rest." Miss. Ernestine gave me a stern look. I looked over at Ezran, who was still sleeping. His mouth was gaping, and drool spilled over his fist, which his head was resting on. I walked over to him and chuckled. I think I woke him, though.

"Hey! Are you laughing at me?" Ezran said tiredly. "Maybe," I cross my arms and fidget with my chin.

"Ms. Ernestine said we gotta leave," I bounced up onto my tip toes.

"Oh, okay, when can we be back?" Ezran asked, stretching out his arms over his head. He made me blush hard."Oh- uh- after lunch, I think." I looked at his feet to try to hide my scarlet-red face.

"Well, I guess that will give us time to clean up. Maybe go check on the dining hall, don't you think?" Ezran said.

"Oh, yeah," I said quietly. I made my way out of the hospital wing doors.

Ezran and I walked toward the dining hall in complete silence. My head buzzed with voices and questions and words I couldn't understand. Why was this happening, who did this, who was the man who stopped me, why, why, why!

"You okay?" Ezran stopped in front of me. "Yeah," I lied.

"Wait, how come I don't need the hospital?"

"A wyvern's claws literally slashed through me! I should have been in two pieces and completely dead right now!" I slid down the marble wall.

Chapter 12

I swung open my dorm room door and saw my bed. It glowed with glory, reminding me of the peace and gentleness that it offered me. How amazing it was to be welcomed by your bed. The bed seemed to be inviting me to give myself over to its comforting sanctuary. I don't even remember putting my head on the pillow.

I woke up to moonlight casting onto Garcia's empty bed. I have flashbacks of the screaming and screeching of her and the wyvern. I remember finding Ajax lying nearly dead in his meadow. I figured this was one of those memories that's hard to shake out of your head.

I looked at the ceiling and saw cobwebs on the beams. I flip my covers over and slowly step onto the cold wood floor. I heard a knock on the door, thinking it was Ezran, but instead, it was Dean Beatrice.

"Hey, Sage, how are you doing?" she asked, walking into my room slowly. She scanned my room quickly, making sure nothing was broken.

"I'm fine, I guess," I say, plopping myself onto Garcia's bed.

"No, are you okay?" Beatrice kneeled in front of me. She took my hand gently. "Yes, I lived in New York City," I giggled.

"Yeah, I don't think New York has deadly-massive dragons flying around and hunting people. Besides, those monsters would get caught up in the middle of some buildings, all tangled up", Dean Beatrice gave a weak laugh.

"True, but New York's sewer rats are no joke." I tried to make the situation better.

"Well, are you hurt," Beatrice rubbed the top of my hand.

"Not anymore," I said, with a bit of pep in my voice.

"Who healed you?"

"Ezran Burgess, roommates with-" Beatrice interrupted me.

"I know who you're talking about, dear," She put her hand up to indicate 'please stop talking.'

"So, did Ezran heal you?" Beatrice asked.

"Yes, I already said that," I said, getting annoyed with the situation. "Okay, good," I stand up off Garcia's bed and pace over to mine.

"Well, visiting hours are not for a few more hours. It's still 1 a.m." Beatrice walked out of my dorm, shooting me a soft smile.

I tossed and turned in my bed. The sight of Garcia's empty bed made my mind ponder about a lot of things that had happened that day. I wasn't able to shake Ezran from my mind. I was hesitant at first but finally decided that I should visit him anyway. I knew I was breaking the rules. But you know what they say, that rules are made to be broken!

I grab my slippers and slide them on my cold feet.

I slowly walked over to my door and leaned down on the handle. I pushed open my door carefully so it wouldn't creak. I tiptoed over to the common room. The blazing fire lit my way as I finally reached Ezran's door. I looked at the metal plaque screwed into the door. It read Burgess, Ezran-Christopher, Ajax.

"Oh," I placed my fingers on Ajax's name. I quietly knocked on his door, and almost instantly, Ezran answered. He wore the same clothes as me, except his shirt, which he wasn't wearing.

"Oh, I was not expecting visitors," Ezran blushed and raced to get a bathrobe.

I squeak quietly as I stare at the wooden floor.

"C-come in," Ezran stuttered as he invited me into his dorm.

I walk in slowly, still frozen inside.

"Sit, please," Ezran waved his hand to a black leather chair similar to the one in the common room. I sat down in front of his fireplace.

"So, what's up?" He rubbed his eyes and sat next to me.

"It's one in the morning. I can't sleep, and I had a crazy idea," I stare blankly into the fire. I found that to be a common habit of mine.

"There's no such thing as a crazy idea," Ezran scratched his calf.

"Anyways, I was thinking we should investigate," I stare Ezran dead in the eyes. "Investigate!" Ezran yelled. He clapped his hand over his mouth.

"Yes, we find the wyverns cave, see if it has a family, and we try to stop it," I say.

Ezran looks in shock.

It's as if he just saw a ghost or something. "You good?" I wave my hand in front of his face jokingly.

"We, we, we WHAT?!" Ezran's eyes roll into the back of his head. I stand up out of the chair and slap him across the face.

"OW!"

"One thing to know about me, never pass out when talking to me," I say jokingly, crossing my legs. "Geeze," Ezran rubbed his cheek.

"But, despite the fact that you just slapped me, I agree to join you on your crazy adventure." He made it sound like a kid's TV show segment.

"Ew, please don't call it my crazy adventure," I make a disgusted face.

Ezran chuckles quietly. We both stared into the fireplace for what seemed like a minute. The sun started to poke behind the hills.

"Ezran, it's sunrise, I have to go." I scrambled out of the seat and ran toward the door when I looked back, and saw Ezran was dead asleep. I smiled softly and walked out of his dorm when I was greeted unexpectedly by one blonde haired boy.

"Hmm, why is the newbie hanging out in Ezran's room?" He leaned down to smile smugly on my face. "Oh, uh," I blanked.

"I was just, uh,"

"Mhm, I know what you were just," He scoffed and pushed me to the side to walk into Ezran's room. "What are you doing?" The boy yelled at Ezran as the door slammed behind him.

"Letting a girl into the boy's wing is NOT allowed!" "She couldn't sleep!" Ezran sounded scared.

"Mhm," something slammed on the floor. I gasped, hoping the boy didn't beat Ezran.

"We wanted to investigate! The dance! The dragon! We want to investigate," Ezran sounded in charge now.

"Whatever, don't let it happen again," I heard the boy's footsteps approaching the door. I race to the common room, grab a book and pretend I've been there the whole time. I see the boy scoff again and walk to his room.

After a few hours of the morning had passed, I went and headed right to the hospital wing. I don't bother knocking on Ezran's door. I just figured he would have common sense to visit. I reach the hospital wing and notice more people fill the beds.

"Oh my," I put my hand over my mouth and surveyed the ward. It looked like a military infirmary.

I looked next to me and saw Ezran standing there. He also had his hand over his mouth.

"All of those people from the dance?" I said quietly. I walked into the ward and found Ajax and Garcia talking through a sheet dividing them. Ajax lay paralyzed, staring at the ceiling.

"Hey sage, thanks for saving me," Ajax smiled and strained to lift his head.

"EHEM! I'm here too!" Garcia yelled at me playfully. She wheeled around the curtain in a wheelchair and legs in plasters.

"Garcia, your legs," I look at her plasters.

"Oh, it's nothing, just a few scratches," she said, flapping her hands. "Uh, yeah, no, you were almost eaten alive!" I yell quietly.

"Ezran, hi!" Garcia wheeled her chair to face Ezran. "Hello," Ezran bowed.

"How are you?"

"I'm okay," Garcia shrugged like her broken legs were nothing.

"We wanted to tell you something," I stood in front of Ajax's bed and projected my voice confidently. "So, the dance, I don't like how it went, so I'm going to investigate—"

"We, we are going to investigate," Ezran narrowed his eyes.

"Yes, we are going to find the wyvern's family and hunt it down!" I raise my fist in the air.

I looked at Ajax and Garcia. Both of their mouths were gaping. "So, how does that apply to us?" Ajax said rudely.

"Well, it doesn't necessarily apply to you, Ajax, being that your limbs are incapable of functioning," Ezran said in a deep professor's voice.

"Good," Ajax relaxed.

"Wait, but how am I going to go? I can't really walk," Garcia smirked. "Well," Ezran walked before me and bent down in front of Gracia. "Sneak out, I can heal you," Ezran whispered.

"Only if you want, you're a good kid," Ezran put his weight on his back foot. "Uh-mh-uh sure," Garcia hesitated.

"Does it hurt?" She asked, scratching her plaster cuff. "Sage?" Ezran looked my way.

"No, it doesn't hurt, but it does tingle for a while," I said.

"Wait? You were hurt!?" Garcia stood out of her chair but quickly fell onto Ajax's bed. "Yes, the-th wyvern's claws slashed through my chest, I don't want to talk about it." I looked at my black buckle shoes.

"And then I came to save you!" Garcia remembered.

"Yep, I don't really remember being saved, but I do remember finding Ajax," I smile softly and look at Ajax's chin.

"On second thought, you should stay here and heal properly with Ajax," I said to Garcia as memories of that night came back to me.

"I also remember...I remember something." My head started to spin,

I fling open the curtain separating Garcia and Ajax and sit on Garcia's bed, trying to figure out why the room is pulsing. I look at Ezran, who's talking, but his voice is drowned out by buzzing sound waves. I glance at Garcia, who is panicking and waving her arms. I groan and fall back onto the bed. I close my eyes and see flashes of people in a carriage. The people reappear only inside a home eating dinner. A black-haired girl with a round face comes close to my memory. She smiles and hugs my memory self. I jolt awake, screaming IVY!

Chapter 13

I awoke slowly to nurses yelling frantically and tapping my shoulders. The room was blurry and buzzing. My eyes had been washed by tears that left their slimy mark on my cheeks. I saw Ezran standing next to me, holding my hand carefully. Like I was bound to break like a doll made of glass. I sobbed softly, my chest pumped up as I slightly coughed. Ezran squeezed my hand harder as I wheezed. I rubbed my eyes with my other hand, and the room became clear again. I looked over at Erzan came in for a hug. He held me a little stronger than a usual hug, so he picked me up off the bed and swung me around. He held me tight as I laughed.

"Finally! A laugh out of you!" Ezran set me down on the bed again. His hand came close to my face and wiped my tears away.

"Hah, I guess," I fidget with my uniform skirt.

"Well, are you okay? Do you want to go to the common room and plan our..." "Amazing adventure," Ezran whispered to me, which made my stomach flutter. "Y-yes, I'm fine," I shivered and got off the bed.

"Good," he smiled.

We started to walk out of the ward when Garcia wheeled over to me,

"Hey, don't forget about us," she said with a sullen look.

"Trust me, I won't. You'll be helping us once you get out of your plasterers and when Ajax can walk again. Ezran and I need to go out so that way we can make sure you and Ajax won't get hurt again. Think of what the wyvern did to you!" I smiled and gave Garcia a hug, she smiled back at me halfheartedly. Ezran and I continued our walk to the common room.

We passed the dining hall, seeing shards of glass and broken windows sitting on the concrete floor. We saw many workers in blue jumpsuits sweeping up the glass. Debris flew around, which made the workers cough and wheeze.

"I'm gonna go get us something warm to drink. Meet me in the common room," Ezran smiled and walked toward the stairs. I looked at the disaster and trudged toward the dining hall. I picked up a broom that was left sitting in one of the corners and started to sweep. I looked down at my feet, not seeing where I was headed. I ran into a man who was bald and had a few missing teeth.

"Sorry, sir," I looked up to see him. He looked strangely familiar." The man stopped sweeping and looked me dead in the eyes.

"Do I know you?" I asked.

"Nope! Just clean up, crew!" He gave me a fake smile. I got a slimy feeling when I looked into his eyes. The man walked away, which gave me the opportunity to slip out of the dining hall.

I brushed off my skirt and walked down the stairs to meet Ezran in the common room. "Hi," I sat down in the chair I always do.

"What took you so long?" Ezran asked, handing me a cup of cocoa.

"I figured I would help out with the sweeping for a bit," I sipped my steaming cocoa, "I was sweeping for a while when I accidentally ran into a man."

"What's so bad about that?" Ezran said, crossing his legs.

"Well, do you remember that man who stopped me before we went to Lucifer Center?" "I think that was him," I said, taking another sip.

"Ew, that man has no business at this school. You should tell Dean Beatrice," Ezran set his cocoa on the coffee table and started to walk up the stairs.

"Hey! Are you coming or not," Ezran smiled and waited on the steps for me. "We are going now?" I started to walk up the stairs.

"We have to plan, so let's take a hike to Ajax's field." We reached the top of the stairs.

"Well, let's talk about what we know," I pushed open the double doors to lead us outside.

"We know that the wyvern had to come over Ajax's field first, before the dining hall," Ezran said.

"Okay, I know that the wyvern had to come from the east. I know about the East as far as the weather is concerned. It is usually rough out there," I said.

"Oh, in my first year here, I studied astronomy. I had a telescope and often pointed it towards the east to study the sky in that direction. I never really saw anything because there were always thunderstorms and dark clouds that would block my view from seeing anything further than the storm itself," Ezran shivered as we continued our stride.

"Okay, lightning storms, thunder shocks, and monsters with wings flying in dense dark clouds. It's perfect," I giggled hysterically. I pulled up my blazer tightly and buttoned all the buttons to keep the heat in. We were going on a mission.

"We didn't pack anything, Erzan. What about food, water and coats?" I shivered again as a crisp gust of wind punched me in the face.

"It's fine, we'll check Ajax's painting shed to see if he has anything. I'm sure he does. It rains a lot here. And if not, I still have some money from when we went to buy stuff for the dance." Erzan held out five dollars and thirty-two cents.

"That won't do us any good. Five bucks won't even get us a couple of bottles of water," I said.

"Yes, it will, five bucks is more than enough!" Ezran protested.

"I lived in New York City, and let me tell you, five bucks won't even buy gum," I smiled and looked out at the cloudy horizon.

"What is New York City?" Ezran looked at me, confused.

"It's my home, it's on a different planet," I said it like it was no big deal.

"Tell me more about this, You Nork City," Ezran said as he picked up his walking speed.

"It's not You Nork, it's New York," I giggled at Ezran's funny pronunciation.

He stared at me, seemingly eager to learn more.

"Well, it's a big city, filled with art and culture and people of all kinds, many languages. It's beautiful at night, the tall buildings light up the sky."

"New York City, also known as the Big Apple. Oh, I almost forgot to mention to you about the pizza there. Straight out of the fire pits, there is no pizza in the world like New York's pizza."

I think blissfully about my used-to-be-home. Then, the memories of Donny's Pit pizza restaurant began to haunt me. I could smell the melted cheese, even though the cold wintery air pushed against us. I didn't realize I missed home so much. I turned my head at Ezran, whose mouth was gaping.

"First and foremost, I must say, that place sounds magical! Secondly, what is a pizza?" Ezran said with a crumpled forehead.

"Pizza is pure heaven. You won't understand until you have it. And while it may seem magical to someone else, to me, it's just a home. A place where I come from. My home world makes me who I am," I said. I looked around the setting, cloudy, cold, and dreary.

A few months ago, I would've thought this place was something out of a movie, but now it's just here, sitting on another planet. It doesn't feel like anything has really changed. Ajax's painting shed came into view as Ezran and I trudged through the mud.

"Ew," Ezran said quietly. He lifted up his foot and saw the nasty mud that stuck to his shoes. I laughed a bit as he was totally disgusted.

"Oh, it's fine, at least it's not pouring down rain," I looked over at Ajax's creek, which was partially frozen by the crisp air.

"Why is Ajax's door open?" I walked toward the door to examine it.

The wooden door hanging off its hinges. A draft flew in from the cracks of the shed, making it even more uncomfortable.

"Okay, Ladies first," Ezran said jokingly. "Okay!" I said confidently.

"Wait, let me come with you," Ezran got up off Ajax's painting rock. "Oh my, this place is a mess," I surveyed the room.

Paint cans spilled all over the floor, canvases were torn on the floor, the easel was knocked over, and the top broke off. A painting laid face down on the easel still.

"What's that?" Ezran crouched down and flipped the painting.

"Oh my, that's beautiful!" I took the painting out of Ezran's hands. I looked at the wonder. A beautiful flower field swayed in the painting. A girl who looked a lot like Garcia danced in the field gracefully. She wore a beautiful white dress that flowed with the still wind.

"This is amazing," I said in awe.

"Yeah, Ajax is pretty talented. I know that because he was my roommate for the past few years. The first year he was here, he brought boxes of sketchbooks. Only sketchbooks. And you know what?" Ezran asked.

"What?" I said.

"He only had one pencil. Just one. When it came up missing one day, he cried like a baby," Ezran laughed and looked at his sketches that splayed messily on the floor.

"One pencil, wow. Boxes of sketchbooks, I wish I was that committed to drawing," I said, running my hands along the collection of sketchbooks on a shelf.

"Well, I'm no detective, but it doesn't look like anything will be useful for our trip, Ezran," I said, crossing my arms.

"Not everything," Ezran shivered and walked toward the shelf beside me. Two pairs of raincoats and boots sat on the bottom shelf.

"Here," he picked up the boots and coat and handed them to me. "Well then, I stand corrected." I put on the yellow coat.

"So where to now?" We walked out of the shed.

"Lucifer center," Ezran said proudly. He had a jump in his step, which gave me a better view of this journey. Sun poked out of the gloomy clouds that covered the sky. The atmosphere became warm and humid, and soon the clouds disappeared.

"Well, hello, sun!" I looked up proudly at the sun. I squinted my eyes so I didn't go blind.

"You like the sun, huh?" Ezran smiled at me.

"Well, yeah. I usually never see it. It's always hidden behind skyscrapers." I widened my arms to make a visual of the buildings jokingly.

"I like the sound of New York, it sounds...I don't know, it just kinda sounds nice." Ezran tipped his chin toward the sun like me.

"Yeah, it's nice. I miss it. It was the irst place I met Ivy," I said quietly. "Ivy?" Ezran and I kept walking.

"She's my friend. She came into my mom's apartment one morning, and a little black kitten made her way into my mom's bed sheets. I went to get some milk and..." I rubbed my head to try and remember more.

"I...she disappeared a few hours later and then came back. When she came back, she was standing there in the form of a girl. She was quite nice. She brought my mom and me to this world that you guys call, *the world in between*".

"Wow, is she nice?" Ezran asked respectfully.

"Yes, the kindest person I knew," I started to get teary, but I didn't let my tears fall.

"That's awesome, it sounds like Ivy was really kind," Ezran smiled and rubbed my shoulder. "What happened to her?" He sounded like she was dead or something.

"She…I don't know," My happiness quickly faded away along with my words.

Neither of us spoke after that. The sentence still floated in the air, waiting to be caught.

Many cottages and cafes came into view. The chatter of couples and families filled the space with joy and laughter.

"This is a beautiful place. I know I already have been here, but it reminds me o when I took a vacation to Colorado. One long flight or sure." I said, looking over at Ezran, who was still smiling proudly.

"What is Colorado?"He asked. Ezran's constant questions were starting to tire me. I had to always explain myself further. But I did it anyway.

"I've never lived in Colorado, but I vacationed there many times."

"Well, It's colorful as heck! The mountains just climb to the sky, and the sunsets look like cotton candy. One of my favorite places was probably Aspen. It's just breathtaking…everything." I was in awe myself. I forgot how beautiful the Earth is.

"Colorado sounds like a kids' candy shop dream," Ezran laughed, and so did I. "Well, where too?" I came to a halt on the cobblestone street.

"Well, we could go to Friggits department store, Beezle's Bugs food shop, Gertie's fine supplies," Ezran listed every single shop name.

"Geez. Well, I guess we could go to the department store. We'll probably find stu there." I started walking toward a massive castle-looking department building. As we were walking, I admired the beautiful cottages for shops, overgrown vines hugged the cottages, and daisies and tulips sprung from soil gaps in the cobblestone walkway.

"We need food. We already have shoes and coats," Ezran stopped in front of the building. "True," I said, so we turned around and walked the opposite way to Beezle's Bugs food shop.

"Ew, why does it stink here?" I covered my nose with my shirt collar. "It's durian fruit," Ezran said.

"Yuck!" I said, making a disgusted face under my shirt.

"It's delicious! They taste like cheesecake!" Ezran walked over to the front counter and ordered the biggest durian fruit in the store.

"Look," Ezran held open one-half of the fruit.

"Wait, that looks really good," I went over to the fruit, picked it up and waltzed out of the store.

"Wait for me!" Ezran slapped thirty cents on the counter and raced out the door.

"Did you pay?" I asked, walking toward a grassy hill near the edge of town. Once I reached the hill, I sat down and started to pluck small pieces of the fruit.

"Hey, slow down. That has to last us for dinner too," Ezran laughed and plucked some of his fruit pieces off.

"Well, I guess I'll stop," I looked at the fruit and saw it was already half eaten.

"Well, do you have a bag or something to put this in?" I asked, wiping the extra durian fruit off my face.

Chapter 14

Ezran came with a plastic bag. We threw our fruit in and finally decided to head off on our journey.

"This valley seems to go on forever," I looked out to the waving hills.

"Definitely deceives you," Ezran said, grinning at the horizon.

"So Sage, I'm going to have to do something to you," Ezran said with worry in his voice.

"Well, what is it?" I said, not worrying about what Ezran will do.

"Never mind," Ezran looked at me sadly. I couldn't take my mind off what he planned to do to me. Was he planning an attack to kill me? Heck, he has already hiked me up so far, in the middle of nowhere. Nobody would hear me even if I screamed at the top of my lungs, nobody would hear me. Nobody would come to my rescue. After all, he was quite rude to me at the beginning of the school year. Who's to say he won't murder me? The sun started to set as Ezran and I got to the top of one of those hills. We neared an edge when Ezran grabbed my shoulder and spun me around to face him. We were eye-to-eye.

He looked furious, the murderer mad-furious.

"Ezran, what are you doing?" The butterflies in my stomach built cocoons and were hiding now. I knew this wouldn't be good.

"Sorry," Ezran brought me close to him as he whispered the word 'sorry' in my ear.

"What?" He whirled me around on the edge of the hill, making me get off balanced. My feet stumbled and slipped.

"EZRAN!" I screamed at the top of my lungs. My feet picked up from underneath me, and now I am falling to my death with no one to catch me. I saw Ezran staring down at me. His face was sullen and helpless.

I grunted and tried with all my might to fly. The green aura appeared, but nothing happened, "Come on!" I screamed and groaned.

I curse as I see the grassy ground, I think one last time of my life, thinking it would be the end. I stopped in mid-flight before smacking the ground and my soul leaving my body. I floated as if I was in the water. I looked around, and the green aura throbbed and pulsed around my hands. I thursted myself up and flew back up to the hill. For the first time, I felt a sense of control. I could do what I wished. At least for now, I was. I flung myself over the cliff of the hill and landed behind Ezran.

"What. The. Heck." I stand up angrily and stomp over to Ezran.

"EZRAN! WHAT THE HECK!" I waved my arms out of pure anger. "I needed to do that," he said softly, looking down the hill.

"NO! YOU REALLY DIDN'T EZRAN! YOU REALLY DIDN'T," My voice was raised, and angry tears filled my eyes. The person whom I loved for almost the entire time I was at this school attempted murder against me in the middle of nowhere.

"I'm sorry," Ezran said quietly.

"That won't help. You attempted murder. I could have died, Ezran! Do you understand?"

Ezran frowned down on the icy dirt as he fiddled around with his shoes.

If I hadn't relaxed and pulled myself together while I was falling, you'd find me like granny's mashed potatoes served on a Sunday afternoon! You wouldn't ever see me again. Ever. No talks. No hugs, nada-"

"I get it! I'm sorry! Sage, but apparently, you got the wrong message here. I meant no harm. But I had no choice either. I had to push you to the edge in order to get you serious enough to activate your power. This was the only possible way, considering our situation." Ezran waved around, reminding me that we were walking in the middle of nowhere and it was ice cold.

So now, if you would stop thinking about what could've happened and focus more on the main objective here. We need to stay alive and think about how we are planning to save millions of other lives. Is that okay with you!?" Ezran barked, echoing a reverberation in the atmosphere. It was like he had a theater-like effect alteration to his voice. I've never seen him so angry before.

"Y-yes," I managed to squeak. The green aura left my body.

"Look, I'm sorry Sage, for what just happened. But I needed you to get that energy up and going Sage." Ezran's warm eyes returned, and his words begged forgiveness. A sense of understanding struck me, and I began to realize that I shouldn't be so quick to jump to conclusions.

I felt the warm sensation coming back, it rushed into my hands, and I felt the energized pulsations. The green glow grew brightly and all around me. My eyes fixed on his. I felt the uplift coming, and I was flying a few feet off the ground before I knew it.

"So, what's the plan, Einstein? And please don't get me nearly killed this time."

"Ein- who?" Ezran shot in frustration and irritation.

"Nobody, what's the plan," I rolled my eyes, remembering that Ezran wouldn't know who Einstein was.

"First, you're going to stop with the whole dying part. Secondly, you will hover above me and stay close. Watch out for anything mysterious, castles, strange objects, or even wyverns. Understand?" Ezran commanded angrily.

"Okay," I put my full attention on anything that a wyvern might be hiding in or around.

I immediately saw many luscious forests and fields. The sun peeked behind the valley hills one last time until it sunk away. The air became cool, and a soft breeze flew through my hair. I looked around my setting and saw only hills, nothing strange or out of the ordinary.

"Do you see anything?" Ezran yelled up at me. "No, not yet," I said, scanning the fields again.

"How about float down and save your energy for a bit later," Ezran said, looking up at me. I slowly flew down back to the ground and walked with Ezran.

"Can you turn off...your light... thingy?" Ezran waved his hands around my green glow. "Not unless you wanna push me off a cliff again," I laughed and dimmed my aura a bit. "Okay," He laughed with me.

I stopped walking and sat down in the middle of the valley.

"What are you doing?" Ezran said, walking back to me.

"Sitting," I looked up at the night sky.

"Want to join me?" I brushed my hand along the grass.

"Sure, we could use a break," Ezran laid down next to me. I did the same.

I observed the night sky. It was as if someone had sprinkled a handful of iridescent opal dust against a black velvet cloak. I sighed under its beauty.

"I'm just gonna rest here for a bit," I closed my eyes tiredly. Ezran's hand brushed against mine, goosebumps enslaved me as his hand grasped mine, and I slowly fell into a deep sleep.

I slowly awoke with cold raindrops sliding down my face. Ezran still lay beside me, holding my hand. I rubbed my eyes with my other hand and wiped away the raindrops.

I looked over at Ezran, who was trying to mask his laughter. I let go of his hand and stretched.

"What's so funny?" I smiled.

"Nothing, nothing," Ezran stood up and groaned. "Mmm, there's something," I stood up as well.

"Did you know you fart in your sleep," Ezran weeezed. "I do not!" I pushed his shoulder playfully.

"Yes, you do!" Ezran laughed.

"Whatever, we need to focus on other things besides human flatulence!" I chuckled and started walking.

"We need to get to the cave, so we should focus," Ezran finally moved on. "Yes, and if we need help, then we will go back to the school." I said.

"Oh! Over there!" Ezran ran in front of me. "What?!" I ran as well.

"A castle! A cave!" We ran and ran until we reached the cave. Raindrops soaked our clothes, my hair was as wet as a swamp, and my shoes were drenched in mud.

"Are we there yet?" I panted.

"Keep going! You can do it," Ezran yelled back at me. The castle seemed to be growing bigger, and so did the cave.

"We're here," Ezran stood in front of the castle, panting like a dog. "Wow, and to think I didn't fly," I was quite proud of that.

"So, I think we have to split up," Ezran said.

"No, no, I am not going into the castle alone," I refused.

"We have to Sage! It's the only way," Ezran didn't seem to be happy either.

85

"You're saying that one of us could die! Ezran, you could be eaten alive by that- that beast!" I pointed toward the cave.

"That might not happen!" Ezran came closer to my face.

"But it could! Then who do I have?! The blonde haired boy across your dorm? He's a jerk!" I ranted.

"How do you think Garcia feels!? Her boyfriend is lying in a hospital ward!" Ezran yelled.

"But at least he's alive," I sobbed. The rain grew heavy, and thunder clapped.

"This is our only option, Sage! So if one of us dies, then that's how it is!" Ezran snapped.

"Fine!" I stomped away from him and marched right up to the castle doors. I looked back at Ezran, who disappeared. I assumed he went off to the cave.

"Whatever, I don't need him," I whispered. Not like anyone would hear me. I pulled on my rain-soaked blazer and pounded on the castle doors.

"Hello!? Anyone home?" no answer.

"Hello?" I screamed louder and pounded harder. Still no answer.

"Hello?" I tried one last time. No answer. I burst into tears and slid down the wooden doors. I rested my head on my arms that rested on my knees. The raindrops slowly turned into snow. White flakes fell down from the sky like a feather floating down from a bird. I looked up at the sky and wiped my tears away. I stood up and pushed open the castle doors.

They creaked and groaned. I looked around and saw dust and cobwebs everywhere. A spiral staircase stood in the middle of the room. A draft came from upstairs, giving me goosebumps.

"Hello?" I quietly walked around the building. Only my echoes bounced off the walls. I walked over to the metal staircase. I set my hand on the frozen railing. The cold chill stung my skin. I walked up the metal stairs and reached the attic. The bitter, frigid, stale air filled the room. I choked on the air a bit.

The scent in the room smelled like roasted gym socks.

The horrible stench stuck to my skin, making me feel claustrophobic. I felt my heart pounding on my chest. I peeked around the corner and saw boxes of dead cow meat. Big, bold words labeled every box.

"What would they need this for?" I whispered. I kept walking and saw immense chains thrown in front of the boxes haphazardly. I jerked my head around and felt a weird paranoia like someone was watching me. I stayed right where I was until I heard sharp footsteps coming my way. I raced down the stairs, trying to beat my own shadow. I swung the door open and saw Ezran racing, too.

"Ezran!"

"Sage!" Ezran and I met each other in the middle of the field.

"I found cow meat boxes and chains, there's someone in there," I squeaked.

"Look," Ezran held out his hand, and crumbled eggshells fell into the white snow. "Well, there goes our evidence," I laughed.

"There's more," Ezran mumbled.

"Let's go, it's cold," I shivered and started toward the village again.

Chapter 15

Ezran and I continued our long walk back to the village, hoping we could catch a ride there. We walked in silence almost the whole way back. The snow stung our faces.

My hair and blazer were wet from the rain and snow, causing them to freeze. My burgundy blazer was now a mix of snowy white and strawberry red. My hair was frozen to the core.

I looked over at Ezran. His fluffy, dirty blonde hair was flat and frozen as well. His blazer was stiff from the rain. Both of our shoes were covered in mud and sticky snow. I looked back behind me and saw the castle was out of sight.

I squinted my eyes and tried to make out the village. A few cottage roofs made a silhouette in the frosty snow.

"T-t-there's the v-village," Ezran stuttered. My teeth chattered, and I nodded slightly. Ezran's lips turned a dark purple, and the tips of my fingers were a slight gray. I could've sworn I had hypothermia.

Ezran and I reached the streets of the village. We walked inside the cafe where we bought the fruit. The same cashier was there and recognized us almost instantly.

"Oh! My dear goodness! You two are frozen to the core! Please sit!" the cashier said kindly. He scraped matches on the side of a box and threw the match inside a brick fireplace.

He went in the back to brew up some cocoa, which melted my insides.

"What were you two young'uns doin' up in that valley? I know for darn sure that's nowhere for you to be explorin'. " the man said, handing us our cocoa. Ezran and I sat in one of the booths closest to the fireplace.

"D-d-do you know the school o-o-over t-there?" Ezran pointed aimlessly behind him.

"Sir Theodore's school? Heck yeah! That's where I went! In fact, my daughter is enrolled there now!" He smiled kindly and sat in a chair that was two times too small for him.

"W-whats her name?" I stuttered and sipped my cocoa. Ezran sat in front of me, still shaking. "Garcia Daniel," the man said proudly.

"R-really, she's my b-best friend there," I cracked a smile. It hurt to move my lips.

"How lovely!" the man grinned.

"Ehem, how are you, young man?" He turned his chair to face Ezran, who was still purple. He stared off into the oak colored table.

"Sir, are you okay?" The man seemed concerned.

"E-Ezran, stop playing," I shook his arm. He didn't move.

"Come, young lady," The man stood up and walked out of the building. I walked with him. "Sir, we need to get Ezran," I said nervously.

"I know, stand back," he snapped his fingers and a similar carriage to the one I rode to Ivy's in appeared in the street.

"You get in, I'll get the boy." The man waved his hands, and I climbed into the carriage. I was soon accompanied by the man and Ezran in his arms.

Ezrans' eyes were stuck open and never blinked.

"Sir Theodore School!" The man banged on the ceiling of the vehicle and off we went.

Once we arrived at the school, I was thawed out and so was Ezran, but he was still out cold. I pushed the carriage door open, my hands shaking anxiously.

"Sage!" Beatrice stood at the mansion gates. "Ezran!" Amos Boyd stood beside Beatrice. "What happened!?" They asked in unison.

"N-no time! Get Ezran to the hospital wing!" I threw open the gates and held them open for the man.

"I'll take him, sir. Thank you so much for your help!" Amos Boyd took Ezran from the man and started off running to the boy's wing.

"Where are you going, Sage?!" Beatrice yelled back at me.

"I'll meet you in the hospital wing! Go ahead!" I paused my running and waved my hands.

I raced to the girl's wing to grab fresh clothes and wash up any scrapes. I pushed the doors open, seeing girls swarming like bees everywhere. But then all the attention spiked to me.

"Move!" I pushed the girls out of my way and flung open my dorm door. I opened my dresser and threw on the warmest hoodie I could find, a new pair of leggings and my skirt.

I ran out of my room again, zoomed up the stairs, around the dining hall, and right to the hospital wing. I saw Garcia standing and Ajax sitting in a wheelchair. Meanwhile, Ezran was in none of the beds.

"Where is Ezran!" I grabbed Garcia's arms nervously, I was still shaking.

"It's okay! Just breathe, in and out," Garcia closed her eyes and took deep breaths, and so did I.

"What's wrong with him?" Ajax asked.

"Well, we went to the valley and tried to find the wyvern. We got into an argument, and then it started snowing, then that turned into a blizzard, and I'm pretty sure Ezran is dead." I cup my hand around my mouth and squeak.

"Oh geez, well, it's okay, who has him?" Ajax assured me.

"Amos," I said, looking around the ward, trying to find Amos and Beatrice.

"Uhm," Garcia, Ajax and I looked around the room, finally spotting Ezran's helpless body.

"There! I'll be back!" I ran over to his bed. Ms. Ernestine stuck an IV drip needle into his arm. His pointer finger had tape around it to monitor his heart rate. The beeping of his heart monitor grew slow.

"36 beats per minute," The doctor checked his watch. "87 beats per minute," the doctor said again.

"It's spiking," I said softly.

Ezran huffed a slight bit. The purple in his lips grew to a pale pink. His face didn't look as flushed anymore.

"Sage?" Ezran whispered hoarsely. "Ezran!" I sit on the bed excitedly. "I'm s-s-sorry," He coughed.

"For what?" I said calmly.

"P-putting you through this," he whispered.

"You didn't put me through anything!" I assured him.

"I almost killed you multiple times, what are you talking about," Ezran grinned. "That doesn't matter, you're the one laying in the hospital bed," I said softly.

"Mhm," he coughed again. I looked at Garcia and Ajax. Garcia pushed Ajax over to Ezran's bed.

"Hey man," Ajax said.

"Hey," Ezran said tiredly.

"Garcia," Ezran whispered. "Yeah," she said calmly.

"Take care of Sage," he looked at me sadly.

"No, Ezran, remember you are not dying, no!" Tears welled up in my eyes as I took Ezran's hand.

"If one of us dies, that's how it'll be," Ezran said softly. He breathed heavily. "No, no!"

"Come on man, hang on," Even Ajax was sad.

"Sage, p-promise me, you will find that beast, you will kill it, you will make the school safer," Ezran choked.

"No! I'm not doing it without you!" I cried.

"You have to Sage, promise me," he whispered. "I promise," I cried.

"I promise," Tears fell from my face onto his blankets. Ezran took his arm and gave me a tight hug.

"Good night, Sage," Ezran said into my hair. I squeezed his hand even tighter until his fingertips lost grasp. His hands fell heavy. I didn't let go, not for a very long time.

"Come on Sage," Garcia tugged on my sweater.

"No,' I cried into Ezran's blanket, still holding onto his hand. "We have to go," Ajax rubbed my back.

"I can't," I sobbed.

"You have to Sage, what did you promise Ezran," Garcia's voice wavered.

"To fight," I said in between a few sniffs.

"Exactly, Sage, you can't do that holding onto something that has gone." Garcia knelt down next to me. I sniffed and stood up. I looked down at Ezrans' bed. He laid dead in my tears. I set his hand down beside him. The nurses came over with the white blanket. Amos Boyd stood next to his bed, watching. I stood next to Garcia and Ajax. I watched the nurses lay the sheet over his dead body.

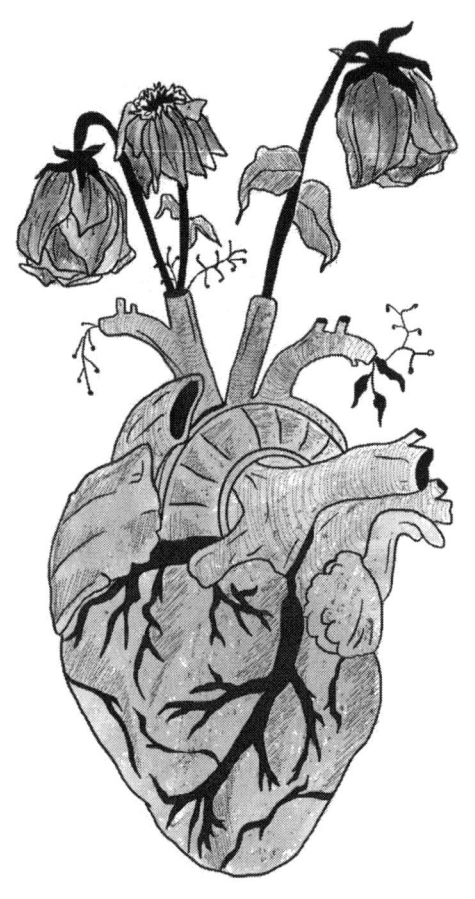

Chapter 16

A few hours after his death, the school community gathered in the dining hall to say goodbye. All of the students were solemn, and the teachers were deep in thought. Once the students sat in their seats, Ezran's family arrived. The gathering went silent, and his parents sat in front of the room. I saw an older girl sitting with them. I assumed she was his sister. He never talked about his family much.

"Thank you for gathering so quickly. The whole community is hurting, and it's lovely for everyone to support each other," Headmaster Louis said. I started to drift away into my own thoughts of loneliness without Ezran. Before I knew it, everyone was quietly leaving the dining hall.

I snapped out of my head and walked over to his parents and the teachers.

"Thank you for being his friend, Miss," Ezran's father shook my hand.

"He talked about you almost every day," his mom smiled and wiped her tears with a tissue. "You meant a lot to him. Thank you for being there for him," Ezran's sister whispered in her chair. She sat behind her parents, looking at her black dress.

"What were you doing out there in such bad weather?" she mumbled accusingly. "It wasn't bad when we left. We just wanted to go for a hike," I lied.

"And all of a sudden, it started to snow?" She stood up and walked over to me.

"We started back as quickly as we could. We tried to find shelter, but it was a long walk back to the village," I looked her in the eyes.

"And how far away were you from this village?" her stinging voice pierced my ear and my heart.

"I-I really am so sorry for your loss. I- I'm needed elsewhere," I stammered and stumbled out of the room. Looking back, I saw Ezran's sister staring me down like a hawk.

I paced over to the common room and saw Garcia and Ajax staring aimlessly into the fireplace.

"Did you come to the service?" I asked, walking over to sit next to Garcia. "Yes, we just left early," Ajax's voice was quavering.

"Ah," I nodded and sat down. Soon, the other boys and girls gathered in the common room as well. Some were not even talking about the service, and some were deep in conversation about how he died.

"Sage," Garcia whispered.

"Yeah,"

"I'm going to help you," she said into the fireplace.

"Let's give it a while. I don't need you freezing as well," I declared.

"I'm gonna go wash up," I started toward my dorm and closed the door.

Once I showered, I walked back to my bed and sat. I checked my watch, and it read 5:30 p.m. "This day could not get any longer," I groaned and slid off my bed. I figured I should participate in communal activities to get my mind off Ezran. I changed into my archery clothes and headed out.

"Where are you going?" Beatrice asked. "Archery," I mumbled.

"It's snowing dreadfully hard! I suggest you do art or something else besides outdoor activities."

"We've already lost one today," Beatrice looked at her shoes. I brushed past her and walked back downstairs. I saw many girls and boys sitting in the common room. More than usual. The room went silent as I walked in. The girls whispered and looked me up and down. The boys chattered loud enough for me to hear them.

"Shut up, it's not like you knew him," I declared and scanned the room. "It's not like you own him," one girl scoffed while others laughed.

"You don't either," my voice stiffened. The boys snickered behind me.

"Stuff it, Sage," the girl stood up, ready to fight. The aura appeared, and I knew that something was gonna happen.

"Hey! Stop this!" Garcia came down the stairs. "Let me tell you the truth, Sadie,"

"Sage was Ezran's best friend, not you, Sage helped Ezran to the hospital, not you, Sage cried on his deathbed, NOT YOU, so stop acting like you own him and just be happy for Sage for taking care of him, do. I. make.

97

that. clear?" Garcia said through gritted teeth. Sadies and Garcia's noses could've touched.

"Fine," Sadie rolled her eyes and stormed to her dorm.

A bell rang and alerted the school it was time for dinner. The sun peeked behind snow-covered mountains.

"Dang," I whisper to myself. Garcia walked into my dorm with a sullen face.

"How are you?" she asked kindly.

"People need to stop asking me that. They already know the answer," I snapped.

"Sage," Garcia hugged me as tears welled in my eyes. I blinked once, and it seemed like an ocean of salty water poured out of my face.

"I wish we hadn't argued," I sobbed.

"You argued?" Garcia let go of the hug.

"Yeah," I sniffled and told her about our two arguments.

"I'm so sorry, Sage," Garcia assured me.

"We should get to the dining commons," She squeezed my hand twice to indicate we should.

"Isn't it a murder scene?" I asked jokingly.

"No, they fixed it up," Garica stopped in front of the door.

"Ah," I nodded, and we both walked out of our dorms, hungry as ever.

—— Chapter 17 ——

Once Garcia and I got to the dining commons, the fantastic food made me weary of its smell. Mashed potatoes, turkey, ham and even a gravy train circled the table.

"Is this Thanksgiving or something?" I asked, surveying the wonderful food and newly decorated room. Circular tables with white table cloths and conversation pits were a new addition to the dining hall.

"They've done this up good!" I ran over to one of the tables. I sat down in the cushy dining chair and dug in.

"Geez! Slow down!" Garcia laughed and cut up her turkey.

"I haven't eaten in two days!" I shoved more potatoes in my mouth.

"Okay," Garcia laughed. I saw the headmaster talking to some of the deans and teachers at the teacher's table.

"What should we do?" the math teacher whispered. "It's still here," another teacher muttered.

"I can feel it," the astronomy teacher agreed.

"I sit up in my tower and see the horrible weather out in the East," he said in a thick Scottish accent.

"What do you think they are talking about?" Garcia asked. "The wyvern?" I questioned.

"Everyone is talking about the wyvern. Oh my gosh!" I dropped my fork. "I have to find Ezran's coat!" I yelled quietly.

"Why?"

"Ezran had found a broken wyvern egg," I pushed my chair.

"Well, let's go," Garcia and I walked quickly out of the dining hall. "We need to get it before Ezran's sister does," I whisper. "What do you mean?" Garcia asked.

"His sister was already hating me. She'll never give me something that personal." I shook my head and kept walking to the nurse's station. "She thinks I killed him," I huffed.

"You didn't," Garcia added as we reached the nurses' station.

"Hello, girls! Shouldn't you be at dinner?" A youthful nurse stood behind a counter.

"We're full, uhm, we need to, uh, get Ezran Burgess's things his parents sent us," I lied.

"Oh, well, let me see what I can do," The nurse pushed open a door that led to a storage area of forgotten things. The nurse returned with a brown paper bag full of Ezran's things.

"Here you go," she handed the bag to me like it was nothing, but to me, it was everything.

"Thank you so much," I said kindly. I peeked in the bag, and the first thing I saw was his coat. "Yes! We got it!" I whispered to Garcia. But the joy didn't last. I handed the bag to Garcia, who hid it behind her back. I heard the piercing footsteps of Ezran's sister.

"We gotta go!" I whispered as I picked up the pace. I looked to see an alternative exit, but the only other hallway was to the morgue.

"Shoot," Garcia and I had no other way but to face our fears and deal with the sister. "What are you two school girls doing down here?" His sister snarled.

"We just.."

"Came to get my friend's things, rest her soul," Garcia interrupted me.

"What's that behind your back?" The sister whirled around to see Ezran's bag. "Who is your friend?" The sister snapped.

"Her name was Nunya," Garcia smiled smugly. "Last name?" The sister came close to our faces.

"Beesnus." Garcia and I laughed and raced up the stairs while Erzan's sister cursed behind us.

"That was close!" I laughed as we got to our dorm. "Hah, yeah," Garcia laughed.

"Okay, are you ready?" I said excitedly.

"Sure," Garcia said. I breathed deeply and peeled off the tape that held the middle of the bag opening together. I felt a sharp sting in my throat as I took out Erzan's jacket.

I reached my hand in his pockets and found crumples of papers.

"You sure it was in his jacket pocket?" Garcia asked.

"I'm sure," I assured her. I reached into the other jacket pocket, and crumpled dust and shells fell into my palm.

"Here it is," I handed Garcia a sliver of the eggshells. "So it had babies?" Garcia questioned.

"At least one," I nodded.

"What else is in the bag?" Garcia peeked in Ezran's bag.

"I don't know, it feels wrong going through Ezran's things,"

"It's not like he's gonna find out," Garcia whispered. I looked in the bag and pulled out some of his school books and journals.

I saw his astronomy book and flipped through his pages. I saw the weather chapter and saw scribbles of writing on the side.

"Take the path past the meadow, head to the village, and hike the valley," I said out loud. "I've been there," I whispered.

"He already knew where to go?" Garcia flipped the other page over.

"I wonder if his family knows," I whispered to myself. "Keep reading," Garcia flapped her hands impatiently.

"Find the black castle, knock on the door, no answer, break-in, chains, cow meat, attic, footsteps, snow-covered cave, egg shells, fire," I repeated that sentence over and over again.

"Hike back through the valley, find Sage, bring her."

"You were a part of this," Garcia shook my shoulders.

"Get Sage, hike through the valley, push her off a cliff, find a castle, fake an argument, go separate ways," I clapped my hand over my mouth.

"He planned this whole trip. He wanted to push me and fly. He wanted to fight and go separate ways," The sting in my throat grew stronger.

"He wanted to use your power even though he already knew the way?" Garcia asked. "I guess, but why did he need me if he has already been there?" I questioned.

"He mentioned the fire in his poem. Maybe he wanted someone to set the place on fire? I don't know," Garcia shook her head.

"No, I don't think so," I flipped through more pages.

"Those are blank pages," Garcia traced her finger around the pages. "Not entirely, there's writing,"

"Well, then, read it," she begged.

"Bella, fire, blood, cherry red snow," I read. "Who do you think Bella is?" Garcia asked.

"I'm guessing his mouth-breathing sister," I scoffed.

"Geez, why do you think she hates him so much?" she asked.

"Maybe because he was born, he became all the attention, plus he had powers. I mean, I would've expected Bella to use her powers against us if she had them," I thought out loud.

"Exactly!" Garcia smacked the floor.

"So now we must figure out how to stop the wyvern and Ezran's family." Garcia declared. "But I still can't figure out if Ezran's family is bad though, like, I met his parents at the ceremony, and they seemed awfully grateful towards me, and then his sister was nearly planning world domination," I crossed my arms and swayed back and forth. Soon enough, we heard a knock on our dorm door.

"Dean Beatrice?" Garcia stood up and answered the door. "Ajax?" We said in unison.

"Hi," Ajax bowed.

"Come in," I scrambled to clean up Ezran's books and the eggshells.

"What's all this?" Ajax asked.

"Evidence, proof, highly dangerous stuff," Garcia teased.

"What do you mean?" he asked.

"Well, you know the wyvern, right?" I asked.

"Yeah, it paralyzed me for a while," he answered.

"Well, Ezran and I went to look for it, but it seems to me like he has already been to the castle and cave and Garcia and I think that his family has something to do with the attack," I stuck my hand in the brown paper bag and pulled out Ezran's astronomy book. I flipped to the weather chapter to show Ajax the steps.

"Take the path past the meadow, head to the village, and hike the valley." he read aloud. "That was the exact place Ezran and I went." I took the book out of Ajax's hands.

"Look here," I pointed to the blank pages with the other steps. "Bella, fire, blood, cherry red snow," Ajax read.

"I think we figured out that Bella is Ezran's sister," I shuddered.

"But I'm still not catching on to the whole 'Ezran's family are menaced' part," Ajax added. "Neither are we. We don't have enough proof from them to fully understand how they might be connected with the wyvern," I announced.

"Which means we have to spy," Garica said excitedly.

"I suppose," I added.

Chapter 18

As night rolled around, Ajax, Garcia, and I snuck up to the astronomy tower with a marker and a few blank sheets of paper.

"Okay, so, I was thinking, Garcia, you shapeshift into an adorable cat and walk up to Ezran's parents and try to distract them. Ajax will go to the castle and cave and howl and make lots of noise and see if anyone or thing seems off to you and me, I will spy on Bella," I jotted down the plans.

"Should I distract her as well?" Garcia asked.

"No, just Ezran's parents, I know she'll take zero interest in you and just sneak off somewhere," I answered.

"And that somewhere is the castle and cave!" Ajax added.

"But the castle and cave are far for someone without powers," Garcia said.

"Well, she could drive or something, I don't know, but one of us has to keep our eyes on Bella," I declared.

"Let's get some rest, and meet me in the courtyard at six a.m. on the dot," I commanded jokingly.

"Then what do we do?" Garcia asked.

"We begin!" I said excitedly. I looked over at Ajax, noticing he hadn't been talking, and I realized he had drawn a perfect portrait of Bella.

"Holy cow Ajax! Did you just draw that?" I asked.

"Yeah, whenever I have paper and a pen, I draw the subject we are talking about without even noticing." he lifted up his artwork. She looked exactly how she did at the ceremony, long brown hair, fox eyes, and a vile smile.

"She seems nice," Ajax laughed at his own drawing.

"Well, let's get some rest," Garcia yawned and walked down the spiraling staircase. Ajax and I followed.

* * *

"WHAT IS THIS GHASTLY NOISE?" Garcia's accent became thick.

"IT'S THREE IN THE BLOODY MORNING!" her Scottish accent made me giggle. I heard a knock on the door, and Dean Beatrice barged in.

"We have another sighting! We are going into a lockdown!" she yelled and ran to the other dorms.

"Do you think it's the babies?" I yelled. "Totaly!" Garcia agreed.

"Should we go out and see what happened this time?" I yelled.

"Sure," I walked over to the door when I realized it was locked from the outside.

"Shoot," Garcia and I tugged on the door handle, and soon the alarm stopped blaring, and Headmaster Louis announced, "All is well now. Please go back to sleep. Your dorms will remain locked until 6:30 in the morning."

"Well, that's not good," I gave up pulling.

"I hope Ajax figures this out," I said under my breath.

"What do you mean?" Garcia lay back down in bed.

"Well, we were supposed to meet at 6:30, so we gotta rush out of our dorms like lightning,"

"He's smart, he'll understand," Garcia yawned and started snoring.

"Wow," I whispered and turned off the lamps.

* * *

Once the sun arose, I jumped out of bed, unlocked the door, and raced out of my dorm. I was rushing so quickly that I almost forgot about Garcia.

"Hey, I think you're missing someone," Ajax told me from the stairs.

"I'll go get her," I laughed awkwardly.

"Garcia, wake up, we have to go!" I whispered loudly and rocked her shoulders. "Go away," Garcia groaned.

"I guess we'll start the trip without you then," I said in a sing-song voice. "FINE, I'm up," she slid out of bed sluggishly.

"Good morning, sleepyhead," Ajax ruffled Garcia's red hair.

"She's a morning person," I replied to Ajax. We headed upstairs and smelled the wondrous aroma of blueberry pancakes and butter.

"We have a minute," Ajax looked at me.

"Fine, only one pancake! We have to get moving!" Our group nearly ran to the dining hall.

Once we had food in our stomachs, we were finally on the path that Ezran and I had been on only a week ago.

"You okay, Sage?" Garcia asked politely. "Yeah," I lied.

"It's just hard walking down this road again, I guess," I replied.

"That's valid," Garcia rubbed my back. It surprised me how much taller I was than her. "You know, you're very tall," Garcia laughed.

"Yeah, I get that," I also laughed. Once laughter filled the scene, it broke the sadness in me. It was still there, but it hung like a cloud instead of a flood drowning me.

"So I brought some money for food and water, none of that weird potion stuff y'all like," I had a motherly tone.

"Okay, mum," Garica replied jokingly.

"So, where exactly are we headed?" Ajax asked.

"Well, we are going to Lucifer Center for supplies and hopefully catch a ride with Garcia's dad. But Ajax, you are going to the castle and watch for anything suspicious. Garcia, you will shapeshift into a small cat or some sort of small cute creature and spy on the Burgess family, and I will spy on Bella," I reviewed the plan with everyone.

"Perfect, and since I'm a part werewolf, I don't need water and normal food, so I can head to the castle now," Ajax pointed his thumb toward the east.

"Okay, I'll meet you there in a day or so," Ajax said, barking and racing on four legs. "Well, you don't see that every day," I told myself.

"Okay, Garcia, let's go to your dad's bakery and ask him for a ride to Bella's house," I said. Thanks to Garcia shapeshifting into a dragon, we reached the bakery in less than a minute.

"Hey Papa," Garica hugged her father.

"Hey, little baker!" her father wrapped her up in a big hug.

"So, Papa, we were wondering if Sage and I could borrow your car," Garcia sounded concerned. "And why?" her father asked.

"We need to go see Ezran's sister, for uh-" "Grieving," I added.

"Oh, Sage, I'm so sorry," Garcia's father squeezed me tight.

"Oh! Well, uhm- how about that car," I coughed and looked down at my shoes.

"Of course! Bring 'er back with the gas full!" Garcia's dad winked and handed me the keys.

"Thanks!" I took the keys and clicked the button. The car drove itself to the bakery. "Are you sure you know how to drive?" Garcia asked me nervously.

"Totally! I drove my dad's car everywhere when I visited his ranch in Montana," I slipped into the driver's seat.

"What is a Montana?" Garcia got in the passenger seat.

"Uh, Earth stuff, it's a lot to explain. Let's drive!" I skidded out of the center and sped all the way to Ezran's house. Garcia looked physically green.

We arrived at a beautiful massive farm with army green trees surrounding the barn. However, not everything was blooming flowers and green trees. I heard screeching and saw sparks of fire blazing behind the farmhouse.

"What is happening?" Garica questioned.

"I...I don't know," I slowly paced to the oak-stained front door. "Well, knock!" Garica sassed.

"Hello?" I knocked on the door.

"Oh! Hello there, Sage," A skinny middle-aged man wearing small oval-shaped glasses answered the door. He looked almost like an older version of Ezran.

"Hello, you must be Ezran's father, am I correct?" I tried to be as polite as I could.

"You are absolutely correct! And who is this young lady here?" The man stuck his hand out in front of Garcia.

"I am Garcia! And you are?" she shook his hand.

"Oh! Do forgive me! I am Oliver Burgess, please come in!" Garcia and I walked into the farmhouse, and it was beautiful. Massive tan beams lined the ceiling while recycled wine bottles complimented the living room with string lights stuffed in them. The kitchen had many plants and herbs by the window, which was a view of a heavenly-looking ocean.

"Your home is beautiful, Mr. Burgess," I surveyed the interior in awe.

"Why, thank you! You'd have to compliment the real artist here, my dear daughter Bella," as if on cue, she walked out of the hallway. Once she made eye contact with us, she dropped her mug, which shattered everywhere.

"You?" she roared.

"You!?" Garcia and I roared back.

"Is there a problem, girls?" Oliver seemed unfazed. "Nope, mmm-mm," we agreed in unison.

"Where are you going at this hour, Bella?" Mr. Burgess checked his watch.

"I need to run a few errands, and I won't be back for a while," I knew exactly where she was going, to the castle.

"Oh, okay, safe travels!" and off Bella went.

"Well, Garcia here was wondering why flames were coming from the backyard! How about you show her that, and I should be on my way!" I pushed Garcia toward Mr. Burgess and scooted away to the front door.

"Sage!" Garcia yelled, but I slammed the front door to drown out the noise. I immediately saw Bella's long black hair flowing behind her. I got in the car, turned over the engine and zoomed off. I soon saw Bella approach the barn and unlocked the door. I barely saw her vehicle until I nearly crashed into a tree. I saw dark clouds begin to form, and so I decided to head to the castle with Ajax and wait.

Once I arrived at the snow-covered cave and castle, I saw a wolf fiercely investigating the setting. I parked the car behind the black castle, opened the back door, and saw fur coats and boots exactly my size. I figured I'd wear the coat if it was offered to me.

"Hey Ajax! You here?" I yelled. I soon heard a howl and a bark in reply.

"How's it coming? Have you found anything?" I walked over to Ajax. He took his claw and wrote the word 'yes' in the snow.

"Show me," I followed Ajax. He led me to the front door of the castle and pushed it open.

"So? It's just a castle. I've seen it before," I rolled my eyes jokingly. Ajax barked and ran up the spiral staircase.

"Oh, up there," I joined Ajax on the stairs. We walked up, but instead of chains and raw meat, there were candles, maps, and books on wyvern anatomy and how to care for them.

"Bella," I whispered to myself. A gust of wind blew and turned out the candles. A pole hit the ground downstairs, and I heard footsteps again.

"Ajax, go turn into a human again," I waved my hand beside him. "Who's that?" Ajax scared me.

"Woah! I think that's Bella," I whispered.

"I think you're right," A sharp female voice echoed in the big castle.

"This is no place for you, creep," I saw her shadow slowly rise up the stairs. "I know you killed my brother, and there's no way of getting out of it."

"My brother was the best in that school, and you had to come in and steal his little heart away," Bella's red fox eyes blazed into my skin.

"He would've still been alive if it wasn't for you, corrupting him with all of your Earthly nonsense about New York and Montana!" she finally reached the top of the stairs, huffing loudly.

"So tell me, brat, why did you kill Ezran?" She came close to my face. "I didn't kill him. He died of hypothermia!" I raised my voice.

"I never wanted him to die. I wish I could've done more," I yelled, and the green aura lit up. My feet lifted off the ground, and I soon was staring Bella down. I looked behind me and saw Ajax was ready to fight as he turned back into a wolf.

"But, the real question here, Bella, is why in the world do you choose to come here? Why is it that you have what seems to be hiding dragons in your backyard, and why is it, Bella, that you are attacking me when I obviously have more power than you ever will? I mean, I can fly and basically snap your neck right now if I wanted to, but I'm not gonna," I crossed my arms and made a sly face.

"Well-you-uh-" Bella stuttered to find words.

"Exactly, princess," I smirked and laughed evilly.

"Well, are we gonna dance? Or are you just gonna sit there gawking at my own self being," I laughed again, and even Ajax was stifling a laugh behind me.

"Never," Bella squeaked. She started throwing fists, and I just flew higher.

I yawned, teasing her. Bella screamed angrily and started jumping to catch me.

"It's not gonna work, princess. Now, what are you doing with the wyverns?" I flipped over onto my stomach.

"If you're trying to get a sob story out of me, it's not happening," Bella crossed her arms and slumped down on the floor.

"Is it maybe because Ezran had powers? Maybe he got into the school, and you didn't?" "Shut up! You don't know my life," Bella yelled.

"Well, I know a lot about people, and it seems to me that's how it is," I flew down a little bit. "Did you just want to feel loved and noticed?" I looked her in the eye.

"Stop it!" Bella tucked her face into her arms.

"I just wanted to have a purpose in my family," She said in her arms.

"I figured that if I started a family business where we raise wyverns and dragons, that might take away the focus from Ezran for once, but now look how that turned out," Bella confessed.

"I couldn't even control them, now Ezran's gone," I heard sobbing behind her sweater.

Maybe I went too far, but I got her to confess anyway. A thud shook the castle and knocked over the candle sticks.

"What was that?" I stopped flying and balanced myself.

"Uhm- well, a few wyverns might be in their teenage years, so they like to start chaos." Bella looked up.

"So that explains the books," I picked up one.

"Sure," she ripped the book out of my hands, and another thud boomed.

"Well, aren't you gonna do something!?" Ajax yelled from the back of the room. "I can't! I raised them, not controlled them, brat," Bella rolled her eyes.

"Hey, is it a little warm in here?" I took off the fur coat.

"Oh shoot," we all rushed to the window, and soon enough, the forest blazed with fire. "It won't be long until it reaches us. We have to go!" I grabbed a bucket that hid behind the books and stools, scooped some snow into it and heated it with a dimly lit candle.

"That's not going to work! You're boiling water! Not making it cold!" Bella ripped the bucket out of my hands.

"Well, if you don't have a plan, how will this work!?" I yelled at her.

"Guys! Stop this! We will get burned alive if we don't leave!" Ajax grabbed mine and Bella's wrists and dragged us down the stairs.

"Get in the car!" Ajax let go of us, and we ran to Garcia's dad's car.

"Ow! Ow! Ow!" I hissed as I sat in the driver's seat.

"The car is heating up! Get out!" We jumped out of the car quick enough to see it burst into flames. The fire soon swallowed the car and spread around the castle and cave.

"The babies!" Bella ran into the cave. "Ajax, what do we do?!" I screamed.

"I can jump over the flames! You go get Bella!" Ajax's nose soon turned fuzzy, and he shrunk to his werewolf size. I trudged through the snow to get Bella.

"Come on! We have to go now!" the cave echoed. The cave was filled with smoke.

"The chains aren't budging!" Bella screamed back at me and rattled the chains. I coughed and wheezed as I lit up my aura and walked through the cave, providing a little light. I took hold of the chains and jiggled the lock, and one baby wyvern was free.

"There's another one over there!" Bella and I ran over to it. I pushed the key into the lock, and off the wyvern went.

"Let's go!!" I dropped the key and ran out of the cave.

"I can take the wyverns up individually, then I can save you!" I yelled and picked up a fallen baby wyvern. I started to lift up and flew to the edge of the fire circle. The flames roared and burned my clothes. I winced and landed in front of Ajax.

"Here," I handed him the wyvern and went off to get the next one.

As I flew over the flames, more and more, my clothes began to burn.

"Bella!! Come on! My clothes are burning, and we still have to save two lives!" I landed inside the circle of fire again.

"You grab the baby wyvern! I'll grab you!" I yelled and picked up Bella like a child. I jumped up, but nothing happened. My aura began to dim, and I fell to the ground weakly.

"Uhm," Bella whimpered and looked around.

"Make me mad! You're good at that!" I said softly. "What?" she yelled.

"Just do it!" I yelled back.

"You killed Ezran! You are a bad person! You are lying down useless, not even trying to help!" Bella yelled.

"Okay! That's enough!" I jumped up, grabbed Bella and the baby wyvern, flew over the flames quickly and landed hard in the snow. I looked behind me and watched as the castle crumpled up into a pile of dust.

"Wow," I sighed and looked at Ajax, Bella, and the two howling wyverns.

"We have to go," I started walking when I realized that my leggings had been burnt to a crisp and my blazer had one sleeve left. My knees had blisters the size of golf balls, and my arms had bright red splotches everywhere.

"Sage! You're face!" Bella cupped her hand over her mouth. "Not funny," I glared at her,"

"No, actually! Sage!" I touched my face and felt welts and blisters everywhere. "Oh god, ow!" I yelled and dumped snow on my face.

"Sage! What in the world!!" Garcia and Mr. Burgess drove up to the fire.

"We saw the smoke and came as soon as we could!" Garcia hugged me, and I cried. "Ow!" I winced.

"Your face! Your legs! Your arms! Girl!" She held my hand and helped me into the red truck that was sitting in the snow. Everyone climbed into the truck, and I breathed deeply to try and take my focus off the pain.

"Drive to the hospital, Mr. Burgess," Garcia said.

"This is a lot like what happened with Ezran. He's too cold, I'm too hot, I tried to save him, and you're saving me, although I have no siblings to defend me if I die," I laughed and looked at Bella. She scoffed and laughed.

Chapter 19

A few weeks after the fire, I stayed with the Burgess's for a while as I recovered. Garcia would come and visit, and so would Ajax and Dean Beatrice. I learned more about Bella and how she started a wyvern farm in her backyard. I was given lots of flowers, but I soon realized I was allergic to them. I got lots of cards and balloons and candy. My legs were still burnt and wrapped up, so I had a wheelchair to get around in. The doctors say I won't be able to walk for a while, but my arms and face are much better.

I have many scars, and my skin looks bleached from healing.

But I would go through it all again to save my friends. I yawned as the sun rose and the birds chirped outside my window. Bella walked in with my wet rags and tangerines.

"Interesting combination," I laughed and sat up in bed.

"Take these and dab your face, and eat your tangerine. It's good for you." Ever since I saved Bella, and we've been living together for a while, she's become a mother-sister to me now. She still calls me a brat, but that's just our friendship.

"Good morning, Sage!" Mrs. Burgess came into my room with oatmeal.

"Good morning, Mrs. Burgess!" I smiled and peeled the tangerine skin. She dabbed my face gently with the cold, wet washcloth. It stung, but not like before.

"Well, I think you will have some visitors today!" Mrs. Burgess fixed her posture and grinned.

"Oh! And another surprise!" Bella ran down the hall to her bedroom and came back with two stick-looking items wrapped in paper.

"Open it!" I ripped the paper open and saw two crutches to walk with.

"Oh! Crutches! I won't be able to use these for a while, though," I looked solemnly at Bella and Mrs. Burgess.

"That's the thing, the doctor called today and said we could start!" Mrs. Burgess took my hands excitedly.

"Really!" I squeaked.

"Yep!" Bella and Mrs. Burgess smiled.

"Well, go get ready! And eat your tangerine!" Bella threw the peel at my face jokingly as she left the room. I leaned back in my bed and looked out at the ocean. I slid into my wheelchair, brushed and braided my hair, put on fresh clothes and rolled out. I came out of my room and saw a gymnastics mat set up in the living room. Butterflies filled my stomach as I wheeled over to it. Two parallel ballet bars stood next to the mat. I wheeled over to the two ends of the bars and put my hands on them to try and stand up. I fell back into the wheelchair almost immediately.

"You need help?" Mrs. Burgess asked kindly.

"Yeah, probably," I said. Mrs. Burgess held my back and guided me upward to the bar. Once I got a hold of both of the bars, I stood there for a while, thinking, "Just take one small step."

I managed to lift my foot an inch off the ground and move it forward.

"Hah! I did it one step!" I excitedly let go of the bar but fell face-first into the gymnastics mat.

"I'm good," I groaned and crawled to my wheelchair.

"That was amazing! Great job!" Bella and Mrs. Burgess clapped.

I tried many times, and each time, I got an extra step and soon made it halfway. I fell quite a lot, but it didn't matter! After lunch, we decided to take a really big step. Outside. No bars.

"This seems a little too much for my first day walking again," I looked out at the ocean.

"Yes, but we will be here. Just take a second," Bella pointed to a rock. I rolled over to it and got the strength to launch myself onto it. I just sat there thinking about everything, really.

Ivy, first, Marly, Mom, Garcia, Ajax... and of course Ezran.

Now, his family is becoming my family. I always reflected on Ezran's words, how he would always say that if one of us had to die, then that's how it was supposed to be. I wondered if he knew what was going to happen that day.

"Well, we may not have what we lost, but...there's always room for something new," Bella joined me on the rock and hugged me.

"This could be a new beginning for all of us," I smiled and looked out onto the sun, sinking into the ghostly gray ocean waves until it became pitch black.

About The Author

Maisie is a middle school student who had a dream to become an Author early in life. Speech came to Maisie at just nine months old and she hasn't stopped telling stories since. Fueled by her love for storytelling, she decided to put pen to paper and the creativity came flowing out of her. When she isn't writing she enjoys drawing, playing with her dog, and experiencing as many new adventures as she can.